# *GROWING UP*

AS TOLD TO

# THOMAS R. CUBA

# *GROWING UP*

## BY THE EARTH WARRIOR

## A STORY FOR CHILDREN OF ANY AGE

TATE PUBLISHING
AND ENTERPRISES, LLC

Published by Tate Publishing & Enterprises, LLC
127 E. Trade Center Terrace | Mustang, Oklahoma 73064 USA
1.888.361.9473 | www.tatepublishing.com

Tate Publishing is committed to excellence in the publishing industry. The company reflects the philosophy established by the founders, based on Psalm 68:11,
*"The Lord gave the word and great was the company of those who published it."*

Book design copyright © 2015 by Tate Publishing, LLC. All rights reserved.
*Cover Art by Thomas R. Cuba*
*Cover design by Nino Carlo Suico*
*Interior design by Angelo Moralde*

Published in the United States of America

ISBN: 978-1-63449-874-6
1. Fiction / Fantasy / General
2. Fiction / Fairy Tales, Folk Tales, Legends & Mythology
15.02.02

# CONTENTS

# Growing Up

There is a long-forgotten tribe of the Great Spirit, which lived long, long ago in the land across the Great Waters. This tribe was once strong and had great magic. The people of the nearby tribes learned some of this magic and began to use it badly.

The people to the west hated the tribe and killed many of them. Others were sent away to live in the woods. Still others went into hiding. Many traveled across the Great Waters to the land they called America.

Among these were the great, great grandparents of a small boy. The boy had many friends, and they taught him many new ways. But the boy thought the ways were old and of no importance.

As the boy grew, he learned many things but understood nothing. When he reached the age when he was to begin his quest, he knew not what to look for. This scared him. One night, when all alone, he prayed to the Great Spirit. He prayed harder than he ever knew he could.

The Great Spirit came to the boy that same night. He came as a tremendous Thunder Storm. The boy asked the Great Spirit what he should do with his life. He asked for guidance.

The Great Spirit said to the boy, "Give me your feet." The boy gave up his feet.

The Great Spirit then said to the boy, "Give me your hands." And the boy gave up his hands.

The Great Spirit then said, "Give me your heart." And the boy gave up his heart.

The Great Spirit took these things that the boy had given him and began to leave.

But the boy called out to him saying, "How can I walk with no feet? How can I hunt with no hands? How can I love with no heart?"

The Great Spirit said to the boy, "You have shown great courage in giving me these feet and hands and this heart. I cannot give them back because you have gifted them to me, and I must not refuse your gift. You may take and use these feet that you have given me. In using my feet, you are certain never to become lost. You may take and use these, my hands, and therefore be certain that whatever you make with them will be good. You may use this heart for all your life. This heart, my heart, is capable of much more than just love. But this you must learn for yourself.

"Whenever you call me, call me with your heart like you have done this night, and I will come. Look for me with your heart, and you will see me. Hear me with your heart, and my voice will be clear as the cry of the eagle."

And so saying, the Great Spirit gifted the boy with the Spirit of the Eagle so that he might soar above the chaos he was born to and see the whole forest and not only the trees.

Many moons had passed when the boy called the Great Spirit to guide him on his path. That night, the Spirit of the West came to the boy. He came in the form of Time. He said the Great Spirit had sent him to help the boy. He took the boy that night and showed him the great achievements of Time. He saw the huge Sequoia trees. He climbed all the great mountains of the west. He saw the Great Waters of the west and the cliffs of the shore. He saw the deserts of the high valleys and the prairies of the plateau. He ran with the Elk that is Time. He cried at the beauty of the canyons among the mountains. His heart had been touched by Time.

When he was returned, the Spirit of the West gifted the boy with the Spirit of the Cougar and took away fear that the boy may never stray from the path of the Great Spirit because he was afraid.

Many more moons had passed when the Spirit of the Forest came to the boy. He came as a Coyote to teach the boy the way of the woods. But the boy had become a hunter of game because he had no fear. He had little wisdom either, and so he shot the Spirit of the Forest.

For three days and three nights, the boy could hear the howling of the Coyote from a hill above his hunting grounds. No matter how hard he searched, he could not track down the wounded Coyote. The boy did not sleep for this time and, through the howling of the Coyote, the boy learned the lessons of the forest. He learned the place of the four-legged people and the place of the two-legged people. When, at the end of the third day, the howling stopped, the boy had become one with the forest, and the Spirit of the Coyote joined him. Because he had been so foolish as to shoot the Coyote, the Great Spirit took from him the hair off the top of his head.

Three summers passed, and the boy was again visited by a powerful spirit. This time it was the Spirit of the South who came to him as a snake. This Spirit stayed with him for five winters and taught him the ways of the animals and the trees and the fish and the birds. He taught the boy the places of each of these, and how they worked together to help each other through difficult times. He learned how each of the animals depended on the other animals for food and shelter, and he learned not to waste.

At the end of their time together, the Snake gifted the boy with the Spirit of the Chameleon so that he may be many things to many peoples. For the chameleon, of all the animals, is never what he appears to be when you can't see him but always what he appears to be when you can see him. He is both truth and lies, but the lies are the ones we tell ourselves.

When the Spirit of the South left him, the boy was quite alone, for he had grown attached to the snake and missed him. He called again on the Great Spirit for a sign to guide the feet he had borrowed. And the Great Spirit answered.

He sent the boy the Spirit of the North who came to him as a great shaggy bear. The Spirit of the North took the boy away to the northernmost forests of the land and gave him a place among the many lakes of the land. He brought the boy many children and put the boy in charge of them. He left the boy and the children alone in the north woods with many dangers. The boy had to feed them and care for them and heal their wounds.

After a time, the Spirit came back and took away the children. The boy had learned over the past seasons to depend on the spirits, and now he had learned how to let others depend on him. It was during this time that the boy had become a young man. The great Bear took the boy home again and gifted him with the Spirit of the Pheasant Hen to guide him whenever he was given others to care for.

He had no sooner returned than a great crow came and took the young man away again.

The crow was the Spirit of the Air, and he taught the young man the special secrets of the great sky. He taught how the rains come and how the sun shines. He taught how the winds blow. The Crow taught him how the People of the Sky live and move from land to land, season after season, never tiring and never losing their way.

This learning allowed the young man to truly appreciate the teachings of his first Spirit guide, the Eagle. Until this time, the Eagle would try to help the young man, but the young man had great difficulty understanding him.

The young man was just getting used to his newfound freedom of the skies when the Spirit of the East appeared to him as a fierce Warrior. The strength of the Warrior Spirit was great, but he taught the young man that in strength is gentleness.

In true strength is the choice not to fight to hurt, but to fight to heal. The Warrior showed the young man the weapons to kill and how to use them quickly and quietly.

He also showed the young man that the most powerful weapons are words and kindness. Words spoken and signs marked on bark can heal and gather peoples of many places to one purpose. Kindness brings the many peoples around you to join in the quest.

During one of the lessons, the Warrior took the young man on a long journey to meet the Great Tortoise that carries the lands through time. The Tortoise showed him all the two-legged peoples of the earth, and he learned the Great Secret of the Spirits that can be told to no one but can be learned by anyone. The Tortoise gifted the young man with the Spirit of the Snail who brought patience to the land.

The Warrior Spirit was not entirely pleased with this gift, for patience can lose battles that need to be won. So it was that the Warrior of the East gifted the man with the Spirit of the Stallion to keep him straining to complete his quest.

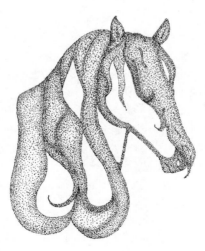

The Warrior Spirit left, and only one moon later, the Spirit of the Great Waters came to him as a worm. The Worm came and stayed with the man for seven summers. He took the man to the Great Waters and showed him the fish, the worms, and all the wet People of the Sea. He learned all the places of these creatures as he had learned the places of the Peoples of the Forest and the Sky. When he left, the Worm gifted the man with the Spirit of the Barracuda so that he may be both graceful and certain in his actions.

The man knew that his travels were now complete. He knew because his heart told him that he was finally ready for his quest. For nineteen winters he had followed the feet of the Great Spirit, and yet he did not yet know where to go or what to do.

He prayed again to the Great Spirit who came to him as a wisp of wind in the night. The Great Spirit said to the man, "Jump blindfolded into the pit where all the two-legged animals of the area come to defecate."

The man lived in the pit for four seasons. During this time he had an opportunity to practice the many lessons he had learned. At the end of the time, he once again sought the Great Spirit with his heart. The Great Spirit came and asked him what it was he wanted to know.

"Is this my quest?" he asked. "To live in this pit of defecation?"

"No," spoke the Spirit. "That was but a test. Here is your quest." But before the Great Spirit gave the man his quest, he gifted him with the Spirit of the Owl so that he might understand. Then he spoke.

"For many years, my people have lived in this land and taken care of it. When the people came from across the

7

waters, the land was broken. The people of your ancestors had been my people too, but had lost their way and now had come to the new land to destroy it. First of all, you must forgive them, for a lost child cannot be blamed for wandering.

"Second you must heal the old people and the new people so that the land can heal itself. For the time is near that the land cannot heal. You must tell all the people that when the land can no longer heal itself, it is not the land that will die, but it is the people who have hurt it who will die. Do not weep for the land, for after the lost people are gone, the land will once again be able to heal. New four-legged people will come to replace the ones killed by the lost people. New trees will grow, but new two-legged people will not come."

The man asked, "How shall I do this great thing?"

The Great Spirit said, "The people had lost their way by not learning the ways of the forest. Much like the boy in his youth had thought the old ways were silly, many people, old and new, had thought so too.

"The people had forgotten how to see with their heart. They had lost respect. Their vision became like granite. You must become the teacher and heal the people by helping them to once again become familiar with the many spirits of the earth. Help them learn the Great Secret of the Spirits that cannot be told. Help them heal each other with their kindness."

"Just one more thing if I may be so bold," spoke the man.

"Why have you chosen me for this task?"

The Great Spirit answered, "I did not choose you.

"You chose me. You called me. You gave me your feet. You gave me your hands. You gave me your heart. They are good hands and good feet. And the heart is the Heart of one of the Great Lost Tribes of the East Over the Waters. If each of the people were to give me gifts such as these, then the earth would not be in danger. And now I tell you that you are now the Earth Warrior. And you are not to be alone. But you shall not be known. It is only what you have done that will be known.

"Go now and do battle. Do a kind and gentle battle using all the gifts that I have given you. Do a battle of encouragement and healing, not of wounding and killing. Teach the people to see with their hearts."

After the Great Spirit had left, the man—the Earth Warrior—wondered aloud how it was that the Great Spirit had given him this quest, for his tribe was not of this land although his clan had been here for seven generations, and he himself was born to it. He wondered why a warrior from the native tribes had not been chosen. It was the Spirit of the Owl that came to him and explained.

"Do not forget that the tribe of your fathers was also a tribe of the Great Spirit even though they lived in the land across the Great Waters. Do not forget that there are many people of the tribes of this land who have lost the sight of their heart. Do not forget that there are many people of the tribes of this land who have granite in their eyes. And do not forget that you are not the only Warrior given this quest of the Great Spirit."

# The Wind and the Leaves

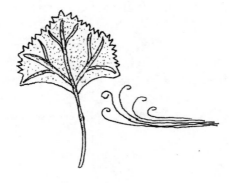

The Earth Warrior had only recently been given his quest by the Great Spirit, and as he walked down his path, he wondered about the true meaning of his quest. How was he to help the people to see in the old way? How was he to even get their attention?

His head told him that this was not possible. There were too many people of too many tribes. There were so many that were blind and had "granite in their eyes."

As his thoughts told him that he could not possibly do this thing, his heart was telling him to simply accept the great task without question. For if the Great Spirit had given him the task, would he not also give him the vision to see the path ahead of him? Would not the Great Spirit also help him to hear when he was called?

His heart told him that the Great Spirit would not show him these answers all at once, but only as they were needed. His heart told him to walk on into the mist even though he could only see the very next step along the way. With each step taken, a new step would appear, and he would not become lost as long as he stayed on the path of his quest.

This struggle between his head and his heart tired him. Looking down the path, he saw that he was coming upon a nice shady spot and decided to sit for a rest of his feet. Beside the path there was a large oak tree. Beneath it the prairie grasses had been cropped short by the antelope. The short grass made a soft place for him.

As he sat, the wind began to stir cooling his face. The soft breezes began to puff and swirl, and soon, the leaves of the oak began to move with the wind and strain at their twigs. The older ones began to loosen themselves from the branches of the oak. With a snap, these leaves jumped from the twigs into the wind.

In the air they danced a wild dance. Swooping like the nighthawk, they plummeted and then rose again on the wind. They shimmered in the morning light and fluttered, spinning down to earth as the breeze relaxed. When the wind returned, they would jump back into the air for another dance.

The Earth Warrior smiled as he watched the scene. It was thankfulness that filled his heart. He thanked the Great Spirit for giving him this little bit of entertainment while he was resting his feet. He laughed as the leaves jumped and bounced and drifted off into the prairie.

He marveled at the magic of the Great Spirit that the leaves contained, for a year ago they were nothing more than dirt and the castings of worms. Then their spirits were drawn up into the roots of the great tree and into the new shoots at the tips of the spring growth.

The buds opened in the spring air, and tiny leaves popped from the bark. As the summer passed, they fed the tree with the nourishment in the sunshine they caught.

When their duty had been done and they had given all they had to the tree, they turned all colors of brown, red, and orange. Now he watched as they danced their final dance and settled to the earth. It would not be long before they were to be eaten by another earthworm.

Perhaps by the next spring, they would once again be tiny leaves stretching from the bark to catch the sun.

As he watched, he drifted off into a light sleep. His sleep was pleasant and unfettered when he realized that he was no longer alone. Standing before him in his dream was his old friend, the Spirit of the Owl.

The Owl spoke to the Earth Warrior, "I see that you have enjoyed the dancing of the leaves. Did you take no lesson from this dance? Remember that in every day, in every encounter, there is a lesson. It is only by learning these lessons that you can proceed down the red road of the Great Spirit."

At once, the Earth Warrior awoke and was startled to see two young people walking towards him along the path. As they approached, he could hear them having an intense discussion over their choices in life. Although he knew not their names, he could see their spirits with his heart. They were the Wolf and the Jay.

They noticed the Earth Warrior sitting in his shade and approached him respectfully, for he was their elder. The young Jay spoke first, "It is clear that you are elder to us and very wise in the way of the earth. We are young, and while our spirits are as close as brothers, we now disagree on our future. We seek your counsel in this matter."

The Earth Warrior smiled at such respect and forthrightness from such a young one and nodded his assent. But it was then the young Wolf who broke into his story with such vigor and conviction that the Earth Warrior knew his mind was strongly set.

"When I grow up, I shall be the greatest of warriors. I owe this to my father and my father's father, for warriors have always come from the sons of my oldest ancestors. The warrior is an honorable and much-needed profession.

"It is the warrior that brings in the food to feed the family. It is only the great warrior, like I shall be, who brings in enough game so that many families may share. I will hunt buffalo every season and bring home meat and skins for all to share. When there are no buffalo, I shall bring home deer and elk.

"Even the rabbits and squirrels shall know my name. It shall be an honor to be hunted by me. I shall be so great a warrior.

"It is the warrior that protects the people from the renegade creatures of the forest. I shall protect my mother and my sister and all the people of the tribe from the marauding cougar or bear that dares to enter our camp."

The Earth Warrior could see that the young Wolf had the conviction and determination brought about by a clear vision of his path and was about to address the youngster when he was caught up short by more of the story.

"I will be the greatest warrior that has ever lived in my village, in my tribe, and, perhaps, even in my whole people. I will be strong and protect all the people of my village from evil warriors of neighboring tribes.

"I will train every day to become strong and wise in the ways of the woods. I shall run ten hills each day. I shall shoot my bow a hundred times each day until I hit a hundred marks for each hundred shots. I shall practice with my knife and my club so that I shall be the quickest and most dangerous warrior of all time."

Just when the Earth Warrior was about to temper this bragging, the young Wolf stopped and quietly but very earnestly said, "But I shall always remember what my dreams have told me. It is in true strength that we find gentleness, and only in true gentleness that there is strength. And so I shall be a kind and helpful warrior as long as there is no one to fight."

The Earth Warrior considered all that the young Wolf had said and saw little wrong which the wisdom of age would not correct in its own time.

Just as he was about to ask them what the argument was about, the young Jay broke the silence.

"I do not wish to be a warrior. I will not fight the fight my young warrior-friend seeks. I will not hunt the buffalo. I will be a great chief.

"I will earn the love and respect of my tribe and my people through the wisdom of my advice. Once they see how strong is my judgment, they will plead with me to become their chief. I will lead my people to safety and success. We shall always move camp ahead of the winter storms. We shall always be near the buffalo and the sweet water. Our horses shall always be healthy and well-cared for. Our medicine will be strong and good.

"I know that to do this, I must study the ways of the woods. I must make many sweats to see the visions of the future of my tribe. I must sacrifice personal desires and give every minute of the day to meditation and conversation with the elders and the spirits so that I may learn my wisdom from all of theirs taken together.

"I also know not to be proud of this wisdom, for it is truly not mine but a collection of the wisdom of my ancestors and my spirit guides. I know that to be proud of my wisdom is false and is no better a fate than eating the poison of the nightshade.

"It is only the wisdom of my ancestors that will let me lead the many warriors of my tribe to camp by the buffalo's grazing grounds. It is this wisdom that will allow me to set my warriors on the enemies of my tribe such that we lose no spirits but take many from those that would harm us or steal our horses.

"I will be the greatest chief our people have ever had."

Suddenly, both the young travelers were completely quiet and looking to the Earth Warrior for an answer. Still a bit uncertain, he asked exactly what it was that was creating the difficulty.

"Each of you has seen your path clearly. Each of your spirits is content with your place. Each path is along the red road of the Great Spirit. Just what is the disagreement about?"

They looked at him in disbelief. "Which is the greater hope?" they asked in unison. "Is it better to be a great warrior or a great chief?"

It was then that he understood the admonition of the Owl to always learn from every experience, for it was in his own relaxed appreciation of the Great Spirit's wisdom that he found the answer for these young ones.

"Come sit with me under this great old tree, and you shall find your answers." he spoke. As the young ones sat, he began his tale.

*Not long ago, as I was walking down a path much like this one, I happened to meet the Spirit of the Wind. At first he was only a gentle breeze on my face, but soon his presence grew strong, and in a burst of dust he appeared to me.*

*"Earth Warrior," he spoke. "I am troubled. I have realized that for all my power, I am as nothing. I am but a ghost pretending to be the Wind."*

*When I asked what he meant by this lack of purpose, the Wind continued.*

*"I am nothing. When I move the wind, it is an act of no substance. When the wind moves, no one can see unless I have the help of my friends. When I blow through the treetops, it is the trees that sing. When I blow along the plains, it is the tall grass that waves to the people of the land. When I blow through the mountains, it is the snow that performs the white sky dance.*

*"When I blow on your face, it is coolness that you feel. When I blow over the waters, it is the waves that place fear in the hearts of men in boats. Even when I blow the great twirling winds of destruction and make the tornado, it is the dust and debris that is seen and feared. I can do nothing on my own accord. I am but a shadow." Having said this, the Wind grew quiet.*

*Just as I was about to make an answer to the Spirit of the Wind, we were interrupted by a slowly falling leaf. It fell ever so gently down to the ground between myself and the Wind. It was odd and therefore caused us pause because it floated straight down. It did not spin. It did not flutter. It only fell. As it settled to the path, from it sprang the Spirit of the Leaves.*

"Now, in case you don't know, it is this Spirit that guides all the leaves of the trees as they begin their journey to the earth each harvest time. She gives them color and makes certain to paint each of the leaves just a little bit differently. She brings joy to the trees and teaches us the lessons of completeness in doing so. But those lessons are for another time."

*"Oh, Earth Warrior," she burst out. "I have lost my feet, and you must help me find them. Did you see how it was that I came to the earth just now? I could not dance. I could not twirl. I could not praise the Great Circle and celebrate the completion of the journey of the leaves. It seems that someone has stolen the wind."*

*Suddenly the Spirit of the Leaves realized that she was not alone with the Earth Warrior. She turned to the Wind and spoke.*

*"Great Spirit of the Wind, why is it that you stand here idle when the world needs you? The oceans have become flat. There is no surf. The grasses stand tall and still. They seem unfriendly to the travelers. The peoples of the earth are sweltering in the heat of the sun. But worst of all, all of my leaves are falling to the ground like rocks.*

*"These gentle small leaves that have worked so hard all summer and have now completed this work are ready to dance a wonderful dance as they leap from the treetops to the earth. You would not deny them such a small pleasure. Would you?" she pleaded.*

*As the two spirits stared into each other's thoughts, I spoke to them.*

"*It seems as though the Spirit of the Leaves has a need of your services. If you did not bring the cool breezes of the harvest time, how will she know it is time to paint the leaves? Without your breezes and gusts, what will the leaves dance upon?*

"*And it also appears that the Wind has need of the Leaves. Without the leaves and the dust and the snow, the wind cannot bring joy to the people of the plains. Without someone to dance with, the Wind is just something to get in our eyes. So while the leaves may wish to dance their best dance, they cannot even break from the twig without the Wind guiding them, choosing their time, and flinging them to the sky.*"

Looking at the two young travelers, the Earth Warrior continued.

"And so it is with all of our spirits. Each of us must accept that we cannot be both the wind and the leaves. We must choose. Will we be the great warrior and hunter that provides for the people or will we be the great chief guiding the people?"

"We must not think less of our friends for having a different path than ours. Like the wind needs the leaves, a chief with no warriors is no chief at all. Whom would he lead? Like the leaves need the wind, a warrior with no chief does not know when to fight or when to hunt. If both wished to be chief, could this be? If both friends desired to be the best warrior, could this be?"

Each of us must ask if we will be the wind or the leaves. We must never forget that without the other, we are as nothing. We must follow our chosen path with our entire mind, body, and spirit acting as one. We must not let our pride get in the way of our respect for our friends and the choices our friends have made."

As the two young ones departed, Earth Warrior realized that the leaves from the oak had also given him the answer to his own struggle. The leaves did not worry over their fate when they leapt from the twigs of the great tree. They only knew it was their time to jump. And so it was the "granite in his own eyes" that had caused him his struggle. By trying to look far down the path and see what the future might hold, he was not able to see the path at his feet.

It was then that the Earth Warrior knew it was much easier and wiser to see the right thing to do right now than it was to see the future. He knew that to be guided by his sense of right and wrong was to be guided down the center of the red road.

He would follow this quest that was given to him by the Great Spirit even when it seemed to be impossible. All that he really needed was enough sight to see his next step along the path.

He knew that to see his path clearly, he must see it with his heart and not with his eyes.

# The Wind in the Mountains

One day as the Earth Warrior traveled along his path, he came upon an Angry Man. As the Angry Man approached, coming down the path in the other direction, the Earth Warrior could see that his very spirit was being consumed by a hatred. The hate had clouded all of his vision and blackened his heart.

The Earth Warrior walked up to the man and placed his hand over the Angry Man's chest. He could feel the thumping of the angry heart through his palm. Startled, the Angry Man stopped his tirade for a moment and looked the Earth Warrior straight in the eye.

Having thus obtained the man's attention, the Earth Warrior spoke, "I will trade you my peace for your anger."

Amazed that someone whom he did not know would care enough to even attempt to calm him, the Angry Man nodded his assent. He was soon to be even further stunned to feel his anger flowing out from his heart and into the palm of this warrior that stood before him.

Peaceful at last, the Man-no-longer-Angry became worried for the warrior. "If you trade me your peace for my anger, will you not suffer tremendously? It is hard enough to carry one's own anger. How hard must it be to carry the anger of others?"

The Earth Warrior smiled back at the Man-no-longer-Angry and said to him, "To take the anger of another is not to own it. For in taking the anger of another, one earns even more peace than one had before. And for you to take my peace and give up your anger is to earn your own peace. It is for this reason that only two angry men can fight. If even one of them holds on to his peace, the fight will end."

Quite pleased with the outcome of what had started out to be a fairly bad day, the Man-no-longer-Angry asked with whom he spoke. Upon learning that he was with the Earth Warrior, he asked for the favor of a story. He asked for a story of how peace was to come to the earth.

The Earth Warrior honored his request, and they both sat in the grass by the side of the path so that they may rest while the story was told.

*Many uncountable winters ago, there lived a young warrior called Belly-of-the-Bear. He was the most fierce warrior that had ever lived. He was tall and strong. His hands were as quick as the very light of day. He was always prepared for any fight that might arise.*

*But he was also a very gentle and warm man. He could remove the splinter from the eyelid of a child with the point of his hunting knife and not cause a tear to fall.*

*And thus he was called Belly-of-the-Bear. For like a bear's big warm soft belly, his tepee was a comfortable place for his friends to lie and relax. But for an enemy to stand before the Belly-of-the-Bear was for that enemy to be surrounded by the fury of his sharp claws and to be in easy striking distance of his huge teeth.*

*But this warrior that all peoples were either in fear of or at ease with had one very great weakness. He longed for the companionship of a woman-person.*

*During his lifetime, he had captured the attention of many women of many tribes. But each time he allowed one of these women to come into his tepee, he was later to learn that they too had been warriors.*

*They had come to him to conquer him and wear him like a feather in their hair. As time went on, he became less trustful of these women-people, and his heart became cold to their charms.*

*His story was a sad story made even sadder by the fact that he had never really wanted to be a warrior at all. For all of his life, from when he was but seven winters, he had wanted to be the simple man that painted the tepees of others.*

*He longed for a time when he could put down his weapons and pick up the paint pot. He would make the most marvelous horses and dogs for the tepees of all of the most important men of the tribe.*

*But in his youth, he had learned that he had been given the gifts of the warrior from the Great Spirit. To deny that he had these gifts would have been dishonorable to himself and disrespectful of the giver. To put these gifts away and not use them to help others would be unforgivable.*

*And so he became the best warrior that he could be. He could only hope that when the Great Spirit sent a new warrior to take his place, he could then become the painter that he desired to be.*

*Until then, he would stand ready to defend his people from all evil.*

*It was for this reason that the women-people of no substance were attracted to him—to conquer him. It was his own gentleness that allowed them to come close enough to eventually hurt him.*

*After many women had become his friend and then departed, he became convinced that the women-people were created by a different spirit than the one who had created the others of the earth. He became convinced that the spirits of the women-people must be kept at a respectable distance from his own spirit lest he become distracted. He did not hate them or despise them for this. He only kept this distance.*

*And yet he could not deny that deep in his spirit rested the need to be close to the spirit of a woman-person.*

*One day, as he walked through the woods in the predawn mist of a summer day, he approached a clearing.*

*There in a grassy spot, beneath where the trees opened their highest branches to let in the sun, was a rather plain-looking young woman dressed all in green. Concerned for her safety, Belly-of-the-Bear approached her and asked how she came to be alone in these woods.*

*She responded that she had been sent to this spot in a quest given to her by the Great Spirit. She would say no more. She did allow Belly-of-the-Bear to provide protection for her from the evil spirits of the woods.*

*Each day he would come to her to see that she was safe, and each night he would watch over her from the hilltop above where she stayed.*

*And each time he approached her, she became less and less plain to look at. Each time she spoke, it was as if his eyes were opened a little more to see her as she was. Each time he saw her, her spirit shined a little brighter through her eyes and her smile. Soon he found himself wondering exactly who this woman of the woods was, and why his heart was looking forward to his daily visit.*

*One day after visiting with her, he found himself softly whispering a "Thank You" to the Great Spirit for sending her on her quest, whatever it was. Yet, he still did not know what purpose that she had to be in the woods.*

*He thought that he would thank her for brightening his day. Being a warrior, he was not exactly well-spoken; but being a painter at heart, he did know the symbols to make the words.*

*He made for her a parfleche to carry her things in and made symbols on the outside that told this story.*

Every so often, a special day comes around.

Early in the morning, usually in the fall,

the air is chilly, you get a cup of hot tea and go outside.

Down to the edge of the creek you walk,

the wet grass tickling your feet.

In the still dawn, the morning birds are just starting to sing.

The air is cool, but the new sun feels warm on your back.

And somehow, you just know that there really is a God,

and you thank Him for this special time.

That day was yesterday, when I was with you,

and I just felt the need to say

Thank You.

*She received his gift and yet said nothing of it. She only said that her quest was still to be completed and asked that he still guard her. And so he did.*

*But still, each day she became brighter and more pleasing to be with. This was truly surprising to Belly-of-the-Bear, for he had long ago given up being close to a woman-person.*

*Since winter was approaching, and the woman in the woods had little in the way of possessions, Belly-of-the-Bear made for her a wrapping to sleep in. He made it of the warmest and softest furs that he had gathered through the year. On its outside he made more symbols.*

*These symbols told the story of how he had enjoyed becoming her friend. He painted this story.*

Getting to know you has been
like a walk in the forest.

Starting down the pathway into the forest,
I step lightly and very slowly.
My eyes need to adjust.

The light is different here.
Filtered through a high cover of green
that moves and shimmers,
light hops from one place to another on the forest floor.

Things that I thought I knew somehow look different.
More beautiful, more interesting,
more vibrant, in this special light.

Around each bend in the forest path
is a new vista of the woods.
Each new experience is like
an entire new world opening up to me.
New scenery, new beauty, new enjoyment.

New in the woods, I try and blend in
so as not to disturb the spirits of the woods.

I move slowly but somehow uncertainly.
I've been in the woods before, but somehow,
these woods are different – enchanted by spirits
of tenderness – yet tough and sure of their place.

The air is moist and full of new smells to tantalize the senses.
The trees have a special scent here.
I can smell the leaves. I can even smell the forest floor.
Somehow being here has elevated all my senses.

Each butterfly that floats past
reminds me of each new expression on your face.
Every one new, and beautiful, and never seen before.
And yet ever so satisfying.

A look into your eyes is like coming around a bend in the path
and surprising a young fawn.
Eyes lock together,
and the gaze virtually flows from one to the other.
An exchange of spirits takes place
and in that single instant, a bond forms.

Deep into the forest is a small brook.
As it flows, it swirls and splashes over the rocks.
It talks softly, but somehow its words
carry more meaning than any ever spoken before.

The enjoyment of being with you is a quiet one.
It surrounds me like the forest
and hugs me like the warm air.
It floats like the song of the warblers high in the trees.

But sometimes, like in the forest
when I may have stepped a little too hard
and startled the woods with the snap of a twig,
I feel I may have startled you.

If I have, I am sorry.
It is just so very pleasant being here in these woods,
that sometimes I lose my sense.

Maybe, if I listen very carefully,
I can hear the forest telling me to stay,
or to quietly walk away.

*He gifted her the sleeping blankets, and while she accepted them with much grace, she made no further mention of it.*

*Belly-of-the-Bear thought that he had somehow insulted her and wished to make amends. So the next day, he approached her in the woods and asked for her forgiveness.*

*"I cannot forgive you for you have done nothing wrong," she responded.*

*"Well at least tell me who you are and why you stay in these woods," he said.*

*"I am called Wind in the Mountains. I am here on the quest given to me by the Great Spirit," was all she said.*

*Frustrated by this simple answer, Belly-of-the-Bear asked, "Why are you called Wind in the Mountains? And what is the nature of your quest?"*

*"My name is gifted to me by the wise Old Man of the Rock, who sees in me the soft and gentle breezes of the wind that blows*

*through the highest tops of the mountains. He sees that while I am gentle, I am relentless and never cease to make my breeze.*

*"It is in this way that the mountains with all of their strength and power are eventually reduced to the dust of the roads in the plains below. It is in this way that the hardness of your heart has been slowly taken from you, and you have seen my spirit as one that you wish to be close to."*

*Belly-of-the-Bear acknowledged in his heart the truth of her words.*

*As she continued, she became aglow in her own spirit. Her eyes and hair sparkled with the fleeting arcs of a pink light. "My quest is now nearly complete."*

*He reached out to take her hand, but she withdrew it saying that their spirits were not to be together and yet were never to be apart.*

*Belly-of-the-Bear began to form a question but stopped when Wind in the Mountains began to fade away into the full glow of her spirit. The pink sparkles, like the first glow of dawn, covered her, and then she and they together burst into as many pieces as there are stars in the sky.*

*Like fireflies, the sparkles flew everywhere and even into the eyes of Belly-of-the-Bear, and he was blinded. But in his blindness, he saw her even more clearly than ever before, for he began to see her with his heart instead of his eyes.*

*He could see her at once as a woman-person and also as a shower of sparkles falling all over the earth. Into each tree, each animal, each human, a tiny sparkle fell.*

*It was at that moment that she turned to him and said, "I have come here because the Great Spirit had not yet completed the creation of this earth and wished to do so. Today, I bring to the earth and to each creature of the earth, the final gift of the*

*Great Spirit, the gift of hope. While none can hold me as their own, each of you can hold me if you hold me together as one.*

*"Someday there will be no more need of the warrior. There will be peace in all men's hearts. It is then that you will paint the tepees. It is then that you will find a woman-person to walk with you.*

*"Do not look for her in a path that crosses your own, but look for her along your own path that you may journey together. Until then, do not let go of the hope that I have given you. For in hope is the relentless persistence of the Wind in the Mountains and the calm strength to prevail over the evil in men's hearts and the evil spirits of the dark places.*

*"In hope is the seed of peace." As her words ended so did her presence for she had faded with the sparkles. And yet she remained in the one sparkle that had entered his own heart.*

*Slowly his eyesight came back to him, and from that day on Belly-of-the-Bear could always see the little sparks of hope in all men and women and even in all the peoples of the forest. He had learned to see others with his heart and not with his eyes alone. He had learned that the tiny spark of hope could light the way to see into the spirits of others. In this way, he did not just see their faces that they painted on themselves like masks. And he understood them.*

*That day he learned that someday there would be a woman companion for him. Knowing that, he was now protected from the distractions that the pretenders would try and cause him. He could be more pure in his own quest.*

The Man-no-longer-Angry was pleased with this story but not quite certain about how it answered his question about how peace was to come to the earth.

And so the Earth Warrior continued.

"In some of our people, this sparkle of Hope has been nurtured by its bearer and has grown into a personal sense of peace. In this peace, others can see a reflection of their own hope. Others can learn to nurture their sparkle. When all the two-legged people of the earth can take their sparkle of Hope and hold it out together to light the way, we will find peace together."

The Man-no-longer-Angry thanked the Earth Warrior and rose to leave. As he did so, the Earth Warrior could see the glow in his heart becoming brighter, and he was pleased.

Quietly, the Earth Warrior thanked the Spirit of Hope. Again.

# The Dream Catcher

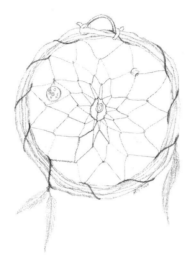

One night, the Earth Warrior lay in a good sleep by the side of his path. He was in a special sleep that he had learned, which was half-sleep and half-meditation. Into that sleep came the far-off crying of a small child. A short time later came the quiet and comforting voice of a young woman. Someone had been having a bad dream.

The next morning as he was about to begin his travels again, a small boy of seven summers came running happily down the road. As small boys will do, he stopped in front of the Earth Warrior and just stared at him, for this boy had not seen a real live warrior in many moons.

As the boy and the warrior stared at each other, Young Mother came hurrying down the path.

"There you are, Little Song. I thought I'd never catch up to you," she said to the boy. "Didn't I ask you to wait for me? And haven't I told you not to run? You might trip and fall down."

Her words broke the spell of the staring contest. The boy looked away to his mother and said, "I didn't go very far. And look who I found."

Young Mother smiled at the Earth Warrior and apologized for her son.

"Please don't apologize for the excitement of youth," he responded. "It passes all too quickly for some. Perhaps this little one will have the good fortune to keep his for a long time."

Young Mother was saddened, "I don't think so. He has not been such a happy child since his father has gone. Today is very much the exception."

"Was that him I heard crying in the night?" asked the Earth Warrior.

"Yes, he had another bad dream. He has had many since his father has gone. I cannot seem to help him with them. Perhaps you might know of a way to rid him of these nightmares."

"I do believe that I can help the two of you," said the Earth Warrior. "I can make for you a dream catcher that will protect you in the night. Sit with me while I make it, and I will tell you the story of another small boy with bad dreams."

"There are many legends of the dream catcher and how it came to be. In one Lakota legend, Iktomi, a spirit guide known as a teacher of wisdom, appears to an old medicine man and helps him learn to see the cycles of life and the forces of good and evil.

"He uses the spider's web to teach this lesson because the strands of the web pull in different directions like good pulls against evil. Iktomi leaves a hole in the center of the web so that bad thoughts may pass through, but good thoughts are captured for the chief to use in leading his people."

While telling this story, the Earth Warrior collected a short length of grapevine from the side of an oak tree and formed it into a circle. Taking some sinew from his pack, he began to thread into the circle the form of a spider's web.

"There is another legend that is better suited for small boys. In this legend, a boy, much as yourself, is troubled by very bad dreams night after night."

*It is again Iktomi that appears to the boy, and again he appears in the form of a spider. Inside the hoop-like rim of an old shield that had lost its cover, Iktomi begins to weave his magical web.*

*As he weaves the web, he explains to the boy that he is making a new shield to protect the boy from his bad dreams. Beginning at the outside, the spider weaves the tight orb of the spider's web so that each dream can be caught upon it and prevented from reaching the sleeper. But to this, the boy protests that he will no longer have his good dreams either. And so, Iktomi places a hole in the center of the web in which he hangs a snail's shell. From the shell, he strings a web strand down to the bottom of the rim and there attaches a feather.*

*He explains to the boy that his good dreams will become trapped and held by the snail's shell where they will become as clear and nourishing as spring waters. They will slip down the thread and onto the feather where they can enter the dreams of the boy.*

*The bad dreams will be caught in the web like the dew of the night and in the morning light will slowly dry away to dust making the web ready for the next night of dreams. In this way, the dream catcher can protect you.*

And as he told this part, the Earth Warrior began to decorate the web with small feathers and to attach a leather piece to the top of the rim so that the boy could hang it in his tepee.

"But the dream catcher that I make is not like either of these. In this dream catcher, like in the other one, the rim is made like that of a shield, and the web is spun in the inside like the web of the spider. In the center of this dream catcher, I will place an object that is a totem of your inner self.

"The good dreams will be allowed to flow easily through this web and give you pleasure during your sleeping time. The bad dreams will also be allowed to go through the web but only after entering this special charm hung in the web.

"In entering this charm, the dream will not be frightening to you. In the morning, it will be held in this charm. When you awake, you will be allowed to look into this charm, into yourself, and remember your dream.

"You will find that in the light of day, your bad dreams are not quite so frightening. This is true of most scary things. In this way, the dream catcher will not save you from having the bad dreams but will hold them for you so that you may understand them. For the greatest protection is in understanding what it is that frightens you."

And so saying, the Earth Warrior finished the dream catcher and asked the boy to produce a special trinket or charm to hang in the web.

The only thing that the boy had was a small round metal charm that his father had given to him before he had left. The boy removed it from his neck and handed it to the Earth Warrior.

Then, as young boys will do, he changed the subject entirely.

"Why is it that you have no hair?"

The Earth Warrior thought for a moment that he was going to have to tell his story of his foolishness with the Spirit of the Forest, but the boy continued.

"You have no hair. My father had no hair. But all the medicine men of our village say that it is wrong to cut ones hair from one's head. Why do you have no hair?"

The Earth Warrior tied the small charm into the web of the Dream Catcher as he told the boy about the legends of hair.

"The peoples of many tribes do not cut their hair because it has the value of having been. You see, in every day that passes, your hair grows a little bit. By not cutting it, we are always reminded that we have a past. Sometimes it is good, sometimes it is bad. But our hair grew a little bit each day of that past, and in it we are reminded that who we are is the total of each day of our past. To cut off our past would be to lose the lessons of the past and to lose our identity.

"But this is also why we braid this hair of our past. Braided, our past is kept close by to remind us of our foolishness and of our greatness. Braided, it is kept out of our eyes so that we may still see our future clearly."

The boy nodded but persisted, "So, why don't you have any hair?"

"Your father and I are warriors. The past of the warrior is not much more than a distraction. In it are his mother and father. His sisters and brothers. His friends and his family.

"For a warrior to be so burdened with the thoughts of those for whom he cares would distract him from his quest. To show total commitment to his work, and his following of the red road of the Great Spirit, the warrior cuts off all of his hair and all of his past.

"And so the warrior seeks to exist only in the present. To do each day the bidding of his chief and not to worry about his own desires.

"This does not mean that he loses any feelings or responsibility to those he holds dear. It only means that his path is clear, and it will be followed even if it takes him away from these personal pleasures of family and loved ones.

"And so, those of us who are warriors like your father and myself, have no hair."

The Earth Warrior finished his story just as he was finishing the Dream Catcher.

"I see that you have watched me closely in making this gift. Because you now know how to make one of these, I must tell you that one must never make a dream catcher for himself. It must always be a gift. For the magic in the dream catcher is held in the fact that one person cares enough to make the gift for another in the first place."

The boy nodded and took the Dream Catcher from the Earth Warrior. After saying his thanks, he left, running back to the tepee of his mother where he hung the Dream Catcher above the place where he slept.

That night, the Earth Warrior did not hear the tears of the frightened child that he had heard the previous night. He knew that his sleep was good.

Very early the next morning, the Earth Warrior awoke to see the young boy standing next to him. He had been quiet. He was just standing there waiting for the Earth Warrior to awaken.

As soon as he did, the boy exploded into a story, "It worked just like you said it would. It really worked. I had the same dream I always have but—"

"Wait"—the Earth Warrior held up his hand—"Is this how you start your day? Have you forgotten all of your manners?"

The young one stopped and politely said, "Good morning, Sir. How was your night?"

The Earth Warrior answered with a smile, "It was fine, thank you. And how did you sleep?"

"It worked just like you said it would. I had the same dream I always have but I wasn't afraid. And this time I could remember the dream when, before, I would always seem to forget it just as I awoke."

"Well, tell it to me," the Earth Warrior said, just as Young Mother joined them.

The young boy sat down and began his tale, "Just as always in my dream, I am a grown man, and sadly, my mother is no longer with me. But I have a woman and two small children of my own.

"As we sit in our tepee, the dogs and horses outside begin to make nervous noises. I go outside and see a warrior from another tribe trying to steal one of my horses.

"I call to him to stop. I call upon his good spirit to allow me to keep my horse. He turns to me, and I can see hate in his eyes. I can see in his eyes the death of my children, the death of my woman, and my own death. I see my tepee in flames, and my dogs running off into the woods.

"And I can do nothing to stop him. I am not wise in the ways of the warrior. I do not hunt. I do not fish. I am a simple farmer of the maize and a gatherer of the herbs. And my last thought is how I have failed as a husband to my woman and a father to my children. And then, I awake."

The Earth Warrior sat and stared at the young child. "Why is it that you have this dream? Did the Dream Catcher that I have gifted to you help you to find this answer?"

"I have been thinking about that," he began. But he stopped suddenly and looked to his mother.

"It is all right to tell the story the Dream Catcher has spoken to you. If telling this story will free you of these nightmares, it is surely good medicine," she said.

"I think that I will grow up and not learn how to hold a knife or a bow. I fear that I will not learn the ways of the forest or the ways of the thief. If I only learn the good and pure things about this earth, how will I recognize an evil spirit when it comes? And how will I protect my loved ones?"

The young mother broke in, "It is true that I do not allow him to handle the knife, for I fear that he will cut himself. And I do not teach him the bow, for I fear he will do harm to himself in an accident."

The Earth Warrior looked to the young mother and said, "It is clear that you love this little one greatly. You love him and wish that no harm would ever come to him.

"But ask yourself these things. If you fear that the water will drown your son, is it better to always keep him from the water, or is it better to teach him to swim? Which would offer him the greatest protection?

"If you fear that your son is clumsy, is it better to have him sit still for his entire life, or is it better to climb a tree with him next to you so that you might teach him each hand and foot movement needed to make him confident, agile, and safe?

"If you fear the bear or the cougar will harm your son, is it better to hide him forever in your tepee, or to teach him the ways of the animals of the woods so that he may never cross an angry path?

"If you fear that the bow and the knife and the weapons of war will cause your son harm, is it better to pretend that these do not exist, or is it better to teach your son to use them properly, wisely, and safely so that these may become his ally in his time of need against the villain of the night?

"Which is the better protection? To hide from the truth of our earth, or to learn the truth so well that your fear turns into respect and understanding?

"One day, as in the day of his dream, you will no longer be here to protect and hide him from this truth. Is it not better to protect him by preparing him for a time when he is to be the protector?"

The young mother began to cry at her foolishness, but the Earth Warrior stopped her. "Do not cry because you love your son. Do not cry for your error. It is not an embarrassment to wish for those you love to be safe. It is not an embarrassment for a young mother like yourself to make an error in these matters. Instead, you should be thankful that the Great Spirit has gifted you and your son with our meeting so that these things may be learned. I know that I am thankful to the Great Spirit for our meeting even more than you could be.

"For our meeting has meant that my work is not yet done and that there is one mother and one child that will know the peace that understanding will bring. For it is in the understanding of mysteries that we are further mystified by the wisdom of the Great Spirit."

Having said this, the Earth Warrior took his knife from his belt and gifted it to the young boy. "This is now your knife. You may not use it until your mother has taught you to care for it, to sharpen it, and to use it."

"Yes, Sir. And thank you, Sir," said the boy as the Earth Warrior began again on his journey.

As he slowly walked down the road, he reflected on how the most important jobs in the world— those of parenthood—are conducted by those with no training. And yet, who is to say that those with training would do better. Did not Young Mother's love for her child allow her to change her ways so that Little Song might have a better life?

And having thought that, he recalled the words of the Spirit of the Owl, who once told him that love is the first step on the red road of the Great Spirit. And once on that road, anything is possible.

# The Dancer in the Road

There came a time when the Earth Warrior had been alone on his path for a many moons. Suddenly, there, before him in the path, was a young maiden. To look at her gave him a curious feeling because he at once knew her and at the same time, somehow he did not.

As she hurried down the path towards him, he could tell that her spirit was in a great turmoil. She came up to him and said that she had been looking for him. Her spirit, which he could see with his heart, had said that she was not running toward him, but that she was instead running away from something else.

Whatever was bothering her did not change the fact that she was a young lady in need of help, and he, after all, was a warrior and was bound to protect her. So he allowed that she could walk alongside him for a while. He would call her Day Flower, for he thought she would not stay with him for very long.

Soon, she was telling him stories of all of the wonderful things she had accomplished in her short life. She went on to advise him of how great a future she had. Their time together was becoming rather enjoyable when they rounded a sharp bend in the path, and were both struck speechless by what they saw.

Day Flower spoke first, in a whisper, "There is the man whom I shall marry."

The Earth Warrior snapped his head from the vision in the road to look at her face. At once he could tell that she and he saw something different in the road ahead.

"Tell me what it is that you see," he said to her.

"I see what you see. I see a tall handsome warrior who is at once both a chief and a medicine man of great power. He is strong. And wise. And a man of great kindness and caring. He is well-respected by his people, and they follow him as if there were no other chief.

"I see him also as a happy warrior, for look and see how he dances in the road. It is only a happy warrior that could be such a great leader and dance like this one does."

And saying this, Day Flower walked up to the man in the road and made his friendship. The Earth Warrior stayed where he was and watched them for a time.

For many days, he watched as Day Flower did the bidding of the dancer in the road. She first gave him all of her possessions. This was not a great amount of wealth, but it represented the very essence of sacrifice. For it included everything she had.

On occasion, she would wander back to where the Earth Warrior had camped by the side of the road. For a time then, they would talk. As the days passed, however, her talk became more vacant and meaningless. Her visits became fewer and fewer. It was probably because she could sense that the Earth Warrior did not see the Dancer in the same way that she did that her visits became even less frequent. She preferred to stay with the Dancer in the Road, for he could pretend along with her.

Soon, Day Flower was working for the Dancer in the Road. She would go to nearby places and barter, bringing back the day's gains to give to the Dancer in the Road. He did not thank her. He believed somehow that she owed him this service.

It was not long before Day Flower had relinquished her own dreams in favor of the Dancer's dreams. She would not return to her studies. It was no longer necessary since she had found her destiny here in the road with this dancer.

She would not have children, for the dancer did not want them to get in the way of his dancing.

She would not become a respected medicine woman. She had hoped to become a helper of others since she was a child of only five winters. Now, she could not imagine how she could ever have any other purpose but to serve the Dancer in the Road.

For three moons, the Earth Warrior camped by the path and watched the young Day Flower enslave herself to this Dancer in the Road. Sometimes he wanted to move on, but he knew in his heart that he must stay. He knew the time must come soon when her eyes would be opened.

He waited only until the end of the season. One day as he watched them from a distance, he saw the Dancer in the Road look away from young Day Flower for only a moment. Another maiden had caught his eye and momentarily distracted him from the spell he had cast over Day Flower.

In that same simple moment in time, she had glanced up at him. By pure accident or by gift of the Great Spirit, she saw him clearly for it was in that moment that the spell was broken.

Her horror was so great, and her shame so tremendous that she did not know whether to run back to her guardian or off into the future alone.

The Earth Warrior stood and captured her gaze. He held out his hand and his heart for a long moment. With a shudder, she ran back to him, and they sat back in the grass by the road.

Neither one spoke for three days. Day Flower spent her days looking at the Dancer in the Road, and the Earth Warrior spent his days making sure she had enough food and water to give her nourishment in this difficult time.

At the end of the third day, as the sun set, she finally spoke, "Did you always see him as I see him now?"

"I cannot be certain. How is it that you see this Dancer with your new eyes?" he responded.

"It is difficult to tell. Not because of the nature of what I see. It is difficult because of my embarrassment. But I know that to accept the truth, I must speak these things aloud."

The Earth Warrior nodded, and she continued. She looked painfully down the road at the Dancer and began to describe what it was that she saw.

"I see a man hanging in a spider's web in the road. No. He hangs above the road. His feet can never touch the road itself, and the spider web is not really a web. It is more like the many threads of the spider attached to the man so that he is like a puppet.

"These spider threads are attached to the man at each of his joints so that his legs and arms bob in the air in grotesque gestures as he bounces uncontrollably. Other threads hold his body up. It is all that he can do to just spin around. His head is also held up by these threads of the spider, but it seems to have a little more freedom of movement.

"The man's clothes are a patchwork wrapping of soft leathers and skins. Even his hands are covered by this wrap. His head is totally hidden by a mask. This mask is a flat white circular shape with two black eye-holes and a round hole for the Dancer to speak through. There is no hole for his nose. Behind the mask, all that is visible is a wild tangle of dark black hair so thick that no piece of the man's head can be seen.

"Above the Dancer, there are thick purple and grey clouds that seem to hang over him, paying no attention to the rest of the clouds of the sky. In the center of this dark cloud is a small yellow glow. This glow stays right above the Dancer's head and seems to grow a little smaller with each bounce of the web. The strands of the web spin skyward and disappear into the purple-gray clouds.

Looking to the Earth Warrior, Day Flower paused and asked, "Who is this Dancer in the Road?"

The Earth Warrior knew that he could not yet tell her. She still must see this for herself. And so he replied, "Who is it that you see?"

After thinking for only a very brief time, she responded, "I must be looking at a great magician. It is only in this way that this Bouncer in the Web could appear as a Dancer in the Road."

Saddened, the Earth Warrior took himself a little away from Day Flower. In parting, he gave her instructions to stay awake all night and sit in the road before the Bouncer in the Web and to watch him closely.

Throughout the night, Day Flower could see the man bobbing in the web and babbling about one great thing after another. After a time, it became clear that even a great warrior and magician could not have done all of the things that he babbled on about. He must not be a magician at all. He must be a teller of tales.

Having come to this conclusion, she looked back to where the Earth Warrior was. He too had a great many stories to tell. Why did he not bob in the road as did this Dancer? Or was it just that she could not see him clearly just as she could not clearly see the Dancer at first?

Having come to this question, Day Flower felt, very suddenly, very alone. She wished for someone that she could count upon. It was then that the Spirit of North Woods came to Day Flower.

Day Flower and the Spirit of the North Woods sat in the middle of the path staring at each other. In one direction hung the Bouncer in the Web, fast asleep. Even in his sleep, however, his arms and legs would twitch from time to time giving the appearance that he still danced.

In the other direction, along the side of the path, lay the Earth Warrior. His sleep was untroubled and he lay as still as a stone.

The Spirit of the North Woods watched as Day Flower looked first one way and then the other along the path and then stared back into her own eyes. Finally, she asked Day Flower what it was that was troubling her.

"Each of these men has strong medicine. Each of these men can make you see things that you would not otherwise see. Each of these men would have me believe that the other is not to be trusted. Where then do I put my trust?"

The Spirit of the North Woods had not been sent to give away answers for free, however, and inquired of Day Flower where it was that she had placed her trust in times past. She was saddened to learn that Day Flower had made a habit of making poor choices when it came to trust.

In her short time, Day Flower had been betrayed over and over again by those whom she had called friend. So it was that the Spirit of the North Woods asked her instead who it was that she had never placed her trust in. She thought about this for quite some time and finally, with a tear in the corner of her eye, she answered, "Myself. I have always trusted others, but I have never trusted myself."

The Spirit of the Woods did not let this end their talk. "Beyond the two-legged people of the Earth are the four-legged people, the winged, people, the water people, and the crawling people of the Earth. Have you never trusted any of these?"

Day Flower realized that she had. She had trusted her horse, Blazing Star. She had trusted the birds that fed on the corn dropped outside her tepee. She had trusted the butterflies to be beautiful each time that she saw them.

She had even trusted the rattling snakes, and the snakes with white in their throats to behave in the manner that the Great Spirit had gifted them. She knew that to come too close was to become a victim, and that this was no more the fault of the snake than it was her fault when she would swat a mosquito.

And it was then that Day Flower realized that her horse had also trusted her. The snakes and the birds had trusted in her to behave as she had been gifted.

It was then that she knew that the people of the forest and the sky and even those of the water could be trusted to act in the way that Creator had instructed them to do. They did not put on false masks and make pretense. And, more importantly, they could not be fooled by those two-legged creatures of the Earth who did.

Day Flower recalled that a while ago, while she was under the spell of the Bouncer in the Road, there had been a time when the Dancer and the Warrior had been together for a moment. A wise woman had come along the path and asked that her horse be painted as she was about to make a gift of it to a special man.

The Dancer had immediately begged to be allowed to paint the horse, for it was an honor to do so. He told of all the horses that he had painted in his past. He told that he was an excellent painter, and that the woman should be honored to have him do this thing. The woman agreed and handed the halter to the Dancer in the Road. The horse, however, bolted and would not allow him to take the rope.

The Earth Warrior calmly reached out and stroked the forehead of the horse, slid his hand down his cheek, and lightly grasped the halter. The horse quieted and stood at his ease.

"I will hold him while you do your painting," said the Earth Warrior. And so it was that the Earth Warrior spoke softly to the horse, who held his front parts still but sidled and hopped his back parts whenever the Dancer came near.

Finally, the work had been completed, and the horse was returned to the woman.

She thanked the Dancer in the Road who then asked to be paid for his trouble and made an excuse about the poor job being due to the unruly horse, and to the Earth Warrior who held him too loosely.

The woman did not pay the Dancer in the Road. She then thanked the Earth Warrior. In return, he thanked her for allowing him to meet such a wonderful animal.

Day Flower knew that the innocence of the horse had allowed him to see the truth in each of these men, and she knew that it was the Dancer in the Road that had made bad medicine. It was also true that the Earth Warrior had great medicine, but that he also had great respect for his fellow creatures and would only use his medicine to help others and not himself.

"The Dancer in the Road is a liar," said Day Flower to the Spirit of the North Woods. "But why is he held as he is?"

The Spirit of the North Woods replied, "Each lie he has told has hidden his true self like the skins of the animals that cover his arms and legs and even his hands and feet.

"His mask hides his face so that none can see his true expressions and feelings. His eyes and mouth are without expression. He has no hole for his nose to breathe with so that he may not even smell his own stench.

"His hair is as tangled as his past. As each day has its own past, the hair that would grow straight on a man that followed a straight path, grows in matted knots on the one that cannot tell his true past from his lies.

"Each lie he has told has tied him to a false place like the spider's threads. These hold his feet up above his path so that he can make no progress no matter how hard he tries. These threads suspend him from the great gray and purple clouds of the death of his spirit. And yet, even as encumbered as he is, there remains a small cloud of yellow above him, for yellow is the color of the self and the only remaining part of his dignity.

"If this liar can stop bouncing long enough to see himself as he has become, he can still cut the thread of the spider, shear his tangled hair, cast off his leather and his mask, and once more continue along his path.

"If he cannot, he will dangle here for all eternity, dancing above a road that he can no longer travel."

The Spirit of the North Woods took Day Flower away with her that night, but not before Day Flower had taken one blossom from her hair and placed it beside where the Earth Warrior slept.

In the morning, the Earth Warrior could see what had happened and prepared to leave. Before he did so, he took his knife and dug a shallow pit near the Bouncer in the Road. Filling this with water, he hoped that one day the liar might see his own true reflection, and rid himself of his affliction.

Neither the Earth Warrior nor Day Flower has seen the Bouncer in the Road again, but they have seen many like him and have become immune to much of this type of medicine.

And so, by having this adventure along their path, each of them can now see liars much more easily and clearly. It is in this way that we can find good things to be learned in even what might seem to be the worst of experiences.

# The Old Man's Medicine Bag

There was a time, not long ago, when the Earth Warrior had returned from his travels to the village of his youth. There, a kindly woman who cared for his son had prepared a special dinner in honor of the boy's seventh summer.

The Earth Warrior had come back for this dinner, for, according to the legends of the Earth Warrior's tribe, it was in the seventh summer that boys were given their medicine bag.

The son, White Fox, was glad to see his father. It was true that he missed him while he was gone, but White Fox knew that the Earth Warrior had much work to do and could not always be in the lodge.

Someday, White Fox hoped that he too could be a warrior of the Great Spirit as was his father. He too would help the peoples of the many tribes of the many places of the earth.

But for today, he was just glad to see him. That night in the lodge, around a fire that smoked from the leaves of the red sage, his father gifted White Fox with his very own medicine bag.

White Fox accepted the gift very solemnly as a medicine bag was a very important part of this tribe's culture. It was the tradition here that each boy's father would make the medicine bag for his son in the seventh summer. It was then that he would no longer be called a boy but would become a young man. That was all that White Fox knew of the tradition or the bag.

No one else would ever let him touch the bag that hung from their necks. That was considered taboo. The medicine in the bag was very personal, and to let another touch it would be to destroy the medicine. At least that's what some people had said.

As White Fox accepted the medicine bag from his father, he noticed how exquisitely it was made. It had a strong leather thong that was woven through the top of the bag making a drawstring that would be difficult even for a rough one, like himself, to break.

It was larger than most of the others he had seen, being nearly as large as his fist. On it were painted small symbols. He recognized the symbol meaning White Fox, his name. He saw the one for his father, the Earth Warrior, and his grandfather, Laughing Brown Bear. The others were a mystery.

While he noticed these things in the excitement of his gift, he also noticed two other things that were curious to him. He already knew enough that he should not ask about these until the guests had left the lodge.

Later, after they were alone, White Fox spoke, "Father, I noticed some things tonight that have caused me to be curious. Could you tell me the answers to my riddles?"

The Earth Warrior smiled the smile that only a loving father has. "What is it that has caught your interest, little one?"

"Well, father," he replied, "I have only two questions. Since I know that your answers can sometimes take more than one breath, that will be enough to keep us occupied for tonight."

The two laughed at this first joke of White Fox as a young man.

"I noticed that the medicine bag that you have gifted to me is empty. When I have seen other fathers give their sons their medicine bags, it has been quite obvious that they were full of one thing or another. They do not let me touch them or look inside. Most of them won't even look inside their own bag, saying that to open it will let out the magic."

"Why is my medicine bag empty?" He finished.

Smiling—because he knew that his answer would indeed take more than one breath—the Earth Warrior began his tale.

*Before it was common practice for men to wear these bags around their neck there lived a young man named Circling Wolf. This youngster had reached the age of fourteen summers when his father had come to him with these instructions.*

*"Circling Wolf. I am not a wise man. I am not a medicine man. I am not a great warrior. I am not a great hunter. I am barely enough of a man to keep my place in this tribe."*

Here the Earth Warrior stopped his story to remind his son that it was acceptable for a man to say these things about himself, even though they were not flattering. A man could say his weakness without shame or embarrassment because there was always more honor to be found in the truth than in false pride. He then continued his story.

*"But I do see more in you than I see in myself. It is possible that one day you could become great in your own way. I am not the one to show you that way. I have already taught you all that I could. It is time for you to find another teacher."*

*"What is it that you would have me do, father?"* replied Circling Wolf.

*"There is none other in this tribe who will teach you the things that I cannot, and so we must rely on the Great Spirit and your own spirit guides to show you the path to your place."*

*Standing then, he pointed across the vast plains to the purple mountains. These mountains rose like the rim of a pan for the grinding of maize from the direction of the sunset. The father said to Circling Wolf. "You must take a journey. A journey from boyhood to manhood. A journey from ignorance to understanding. A journey away from the plain teachings that I can give you and towards the great teachings of the spirit guides.*

*"I want you to go to the top of that mountain that has the red rock in its side. Go there and return. Do not hurry. Do not fear the unknown. For I have had a dream, and my spirit guide has explained this to me as the only way that you can be free of the limits of my teachings and become wise in the ways of the land."*

*Circling Wolf did not truly understand all that was said, but he did understand that his father put a lot of trust in his spirit guides and that to argue was hopeless. "I will go, but only if I may share the lessons of my journey with you when I return."*

*And so the deal was struck. The next dawn, under a flaming red sky, Circling Wolf began his walk to the mountains.*

*At the end of his first day, he had traveled far to the setting sun, but the mountain seemed no closer. At the end of a second day of walking the entire day, the mountain still seemed no closer. At the end of the third day of walking from sunrise to sunset, the mountain still seemed no closer. And so on the fourth day, he paused to reflect on this.*

*Sitting by the banks of a small stream, he pondered the mountain and how near it seemed, and yet how it seemed to walk away from him as fast as he could walk towards it.*

*As he sat and watched, he saw a great ice shelf give way along the crest of the mountain. A huge mass of ice and snow crashed down the face of the mountain. It was so far away that he could not hear it. He only saw it happen. He wondered about this but thought little more about it.*

*For three days, he camped in the plains. Here he spent his time watching the prairie dogs and how they built their homes in the earth. He watched them as they watched over each other. He learned how they worked together to avoid being eaten by the hawk and the eagle.*

*He learned also that if he placed a snare at the edge of their hole during the night, that in the morning he could capture one who was looking up into the sky for an eagle when he should have been looking at the earth for his snare. For these three days he learned much of the prairie dog, the eagle, and what grasses made the meat of this little creature taste better in his mouth.*

*It was on the morning of the fourth day that he noticed that the water in the creek had suddenly become quite cold. As he wondered about this new lesson, chunks of ice began floating past him. He slowly looked to the setting sun and the mountains. He had almost forgotten about them, but now he knew that the ice he saw crash from them three days ago had fallen into the creek where it flowed between their feet, and it only now was arriving at his camp.*

*He watched the water flow and guessed that it moved about twice as fast as he would normally walk. If it took three days for the ice to reach him, the mountains then must be a walk of six-days into the setting sun.*

*The next day, with a new resolve, he began his walk to the mountains. For four days he walked, and they finally seemed to be getting a little bit closer.*

*It was then that he happened across a large brown bear and her cub. He fell instantly to the ground for he had been told that these brown bears were much more ferocious than the black ones in the woods across the great river from his tribe's village.*

*From where he lay in the grass, he could smell the bear. Her scent was carried gently by the breezes that made the grass dance. What he did not smell was the cougar. He had not yet seen the cougar either, but as he watched, he saw the grass move in a way that the wind did not make. Suddenly he could pick out the shape of Cougar concealed in the grass where he hid from Mother Bear.*

*As he watched, he could see Cougar tense up as Cub got closer, and then relax as he moved away. But always, great Mother Bear was there as well. Would Cougar attack Cub? Would Mother Bear kill Cougar? Why did Mother Bear smell so terribly, and Cougar and Cub not smell at all?*

*Eventually, Mother Bear and Cub wandered off into the bushes, and Cougar caught a groundhog. That night, Circling Wolf lie awake under the stars and thought of all these things he had learned, and he had not even gotten to the mountains yet.*

*He would have a difficult time remembering all these tales to tell his father.*

*In his sleep that night, Circling Wolf's spirit guide came to him as a chipmunk. He said nothing. But in his dream, the chipmunk hustled from one place to another, packing nuts in his cheeks. Then he left Circling Wolf to dream.*

*In the morning, Circling Wolf took the skin of one of his prairie dogs and sewed it into a bag. Taking the sinew and weaving a thong from it, he hung the bag from his neck. Into it he placed a pebble from the stream. He chose a small stone with a purple hue to it to remind him of the mountains. This stone would remind him of the lesson of walking and not giving up. It is thus that purple became the color of patience and persistence.*

*He also placed into the bag one tooth of a prairie dog to remind him of how they whistled through these teeth to warn their friends of the eagle. From this tooth he would be reminded of the lessons of working together and of what happens when you fail to avoid snares because you look too much in one direction.*

*Then he placed into the bag a piece of hair that he pulled from the blackberries where the bears were eating. In this way, he would be reminded of the mother bear protecting her cub and would remember the lesson of why the bear smelled and the cougar did not.*

*And so as his journey went on through three moons, Circling Wolf learned the lessons of respect from the snake that rattles. He learned the lessons of pride from the vulture. He learned the lessons of confidence from the goat.*

*He learned the lessons of the prairies, the hills, the mountains, and all the four-legged peoples that lived there. And he learned the lessons of the red rock in the side of the mountain. But those stories are for other times.*

*And with each lesson learned, he would put a small totem into his bag so that he may recall that lesson.*

*Once he returned home, he spent many nights with his father and his brothers going through the totems in his bag and telling the stories that each had, teaching these lessons to his family.*

*As he told these stories, he and his family learned another important lesson. These stories were good for the brothers to hear, but it was also true that these lessons would be learned much better if the brothers had taken the trip on their own.*

*It was agreed that night that the stories were good to tell, but the totems in the bag were to be personal reminders and not to be shared with the others of the tribe. It was also agreed that others should be encouraged to learn their own lessons and fill their own bags with their own totems.*

*And so the father made each of his sons a bag, and each of them in his turn went on his own journey. One went to the mountains. Another went into the rising sun to seek wisdom from the forests. Another went down the river to seek the wisdom of the warm places. The last went to the north to learn the lessons of the frozen lands.*

*Circling Wolf took many other trips as well. By the time he had returned from these journeys, he had learned many things and soon became honored by the rest of his tribe as a medicine man of great wisdom. It had also become his habit to never remove his bag from around his neck. In this way, his lessons were always with him.*

*By the time that Circling Wolf was an old man, he had been chief for many winters. He had developed a habit of clutching his bag and closing his eyes before each decision that his people asked of him.*

*It had not taken him long before he could recall the lessons in his bag by simply feeling his bag and the shapes within it. This is what he was doing when he held his bag in his hands as he made his choices.*

*He was only feeling the totems and remembering the lessons of his youth, but the people thought he was making big medicine and so it became known as a medicine bag.*

"The taboos that you have learned from your friends are the myths made from the truth. The bag is never opened to others, but not because the magic will leave. The bag is worn night and day, but not because the protection might be lost. These are the make believe reasons given by those that cannot understand the truth or are too lazy to fill their own bags with their own lessons.

"Circling Wolf tried to teach the real meaning of the medicine bag, but not all of his tribe would listen. Some, like my grandfather's grandfather, learned the true meaning of the bag. Others preferred to believe in the magic of friendly spirits.

"I have given you an empty bag so that you may fill it with the lessons of your youth, which will guide you into old age. I have done this because, while it is true that the spirits have been known to come to our aid and intervene on our behalf, the best medicine is to learn your lessons and understand the earth that the Great Spirit has provided for us. In this understanding of the earth and of the Great Spirit, lies the wisdom and the medicine to be great wherever your path may lead you."

"That was a very good story, father," said White Fox. He gave his father another piece of meat from the deer leftover from the dinner and continued, "So, why is it that you only wear yours some of the time?"

"Well, that's a pretty good question," replied the Earth Warrior. "Why do you think I don't wear one?"

"Well, I know you have one. You're wearing it tonight. But that was why I noticed that you don't wear it all of the time," White Fox answered. "When I saw it on you for the special dinner tonight, I realized that you sometimes wear it and most of the time, you don't. The only thing that I can think of is that you have another way of remembering your lessons."

"You are correct, little one. In my medicine bag are small tokens of very special times in my life. There is a pebble from the side of the river where you were born. There is a wooden bead that I carved from a tree that grew near where my father's spirit passed.

"My lessons, as an Earth Warrior, are not to be forgotten, because they are always with me. How can I forget the lessons of the sun and the shade when the oak tree is right here to remind me? How can I forget the lesson of the raccoon, when his tracks are all along the river bank?

"Each bird that I see, each fish that I catch, each stone that I pick up, each tree in the forest, the very forest itself, the river, the grasses, each of these are my totems and are all around me every day. When I need an answer to my questions, it can usually be found by asking the next spirit that happens to pass.

"It is in this way the spirit guides have sent me the vision for my choices."

Having said that, the father and the son slept the peaceful sleep of two men who understood each other.

# The Broken Arrow

The Earth Warrior had been on his path for quite some time and had tired. At the same moment that he realized that he needed a rest and some refreshment, he came upon five travelers who had stopped beside the path to have their own meals.

Once, this type of a coincidence would have seemed strange to him, but he had become accustomed to the Great Spirit providing an opportunity at precisely the right moment.

The travelers were three men, a woman, and a small boy of seven summers. Since he was really rather tired, he walked up and asked if it would be alright if he were to share the clearing where they were resting.

They were about to turn him away when one of the men recognized him.

"Wait," he said, "You're that Earth Warrior fellow, aren't you?" Without waiting for a reply, he turned to the other three. "This guy tells some great stories. Let's trade him a place in our clearing for a story."

The other three nodded, and the Earth Warrior indicated his acceptance of the offer by taking his seat in the grass. "What would you like to learn today?" he asked.

The fat man chuckled. "We don't want to learn anything. We just want to hear a story."

The first man slapped the fat man's arm. "His stories always have morals. That's why they're so good." Turning to the third man, he said, "You pick a topic."

The third man, a handsome young man, had been occupied by his thoughts of the fall festival and what he could get as presents for his two sons. Taken off guard, he waved his hand and blurted, "Toys. Tell us about toys."

The Earth Warrior nodded. "I know just the story for the four of you. It is called The Broken Arrow."

*Limping Dog was a young boy of ten summers when he hurt his foot in a gopher hole. He had been running after his older brother during a hunting game and had failed to see the hole. Before his accident, he had been called Summer Sky because of his pure nature. After the accident, however, he had fallen into relying on others to tend after him. Even after his leg had healed, he would sometimes feign weakness to get others to carry out his chores for him. After a while, the others caught on to his trickery and named him for the begging dog that fakes a limp to get extra food.*

*Still, his older brother sometimes felt that it was somehow his fault that Limping Dog had hurt his leg and had fallen into bad habits. And so it was that when his brother, who was called Gentle White Bear, had to leave, he wanted to do something special for his brother.*

The fat man interrupted. "What kind of name is Gentle White Bear?"

The first man smacked him on the arm again. "Don't interrupt. If it's important to the story, he'll tell you. Otherwise, it doesn't matter."

The Earth Warrior nodded to the fat man and then to the first man. "It is important that we know the Gentle White Bear, but perhaps not for the reason that you may think."

*Gentle White Bear was a very large and powerful man of nearly twenty-three winters when he was called away. He was faster than the antelope and thick in his chest as the buffalo, but it was the strength of his character that had earned him the name of the Bear.*

*He was also pure of heart and always thinking of how to be ready for the future and protecting others in his family. For this he earned the name of the White season. Above all else, he was as gentle with his friends and family as he was strong against his enemies.*

*He was the truth in the old saying that in strength alone lies true gentleness, and in gentleness lies true strength. Now he was called away by his chief to help the clan to the south, for they were being attacked by marauders.*

*Of course Limping Dog idolized Gentle White Bear. He was everything that Limping Dog wished he could be. He was everything that Limping Dog could not become until he had found a way to rid himself of his limp, which had persisted even though the pain was gone. And so, Limping Dog was consumed by both his respect for Gentle White Bear, and by his jealousy.*

*Limping Dog was overjoyed when Gentle White Bear was called away because, as his best friend and brother, Limping Dog thought that he could act somewhat on his behalf while he was gone. This would give him the power that he could not earn on his own because of his limp. He became even more excited when Gentle White Bear came to him the night before he left and sat with him at the fire.*

*There, in front of all of the family and all of the other lesser warriors of the clan, Gentle White Bear gave to Limping Dog the care of all his possessions.*

*"I give you these things of mine," Gentle White Bear said, "because I alone remember how you were before your accident. I ask you to remember also and return to the Summer Sky you once were. Be pure of heart and you will find your place.*

*Until I return, I give you these special things. Here is my spare knife. Keep it sharp and it will protect you. Here is my bow and my arrows that I have used since I was but your age. My new bow, that is as strong as I am, must come with me.*

*Keep my knife and my bow safe for I wish one day to give them to my own children. But while I am gone, you may keep them as your own. Along with these gifts, I give you the care of my family and my friends. Let no harm come to them."*

*Limping Dog accepted the gifts with delirious delight in his eyes. He now had the bow and arrows of the greatest warrior of the clan. He had his knife. He had been placed in charge.*

*What none of them suspected was how long Gentle White Bear would be gone. It would be many summers before he would return.*

*In the first summer, the foolish Limping Dog broke the arrows by shooting them at rocks. Others he would leave out* in the prairie at night where the dampness would make them soft. Then, when they were found again and brought back to the lodge, they were dried too close to the fire and curled into half circles.

Limping Dog used the knife to pry apart bones and to lift rocks from the creek. He never sharpened it and never ever took the time to put bear fat on it. By the end of the second summer, it had crumbled to a stump that was used to pound stakes into the ground.

By the end of the third summer, the bow that had been so strong and true had become cracked and splintered through abuse and misuse. Eventually it was thrown into the fire on a cold night.

By the end of four summers, Limping Dog had led his clan into the very pit of poverty. He had used his power over them to claim the best of their efforts for himself. His leadership had given them habits that had bred disease in their bodies and disrespect in the minds of the other clans.

And all of this was done in the name of the Gentle White Bear and the power that he had left with Limping Dog. Limping Dog even claimed that he could speak with Gentle White Bear during his special sweats and his visions.

He fooled the clan into believing that all of the things that were happening were because of an evil in the world beyond their control. All the bad things that were happening were nothing more than a test of their will that the Great Spirit had sent upon them.

One day, Gentle White Bear walked over the rise to the west and back into the lodge that was his so many years ago.

Everyone was overjoyed to see him. He had not changed a bit. In his four summers, he had taken care of himself and remained as strong and full of life as he had been the day he *had left. He was surprised to see the disrepair of the village and the poor nature of the surroundings. Entering the lodge, he saw Limping Dog relaxing before the fire and eating meat from a fat elk.*

*"I have returned, Limping Dog."*

*Limping Dog's eyes almost exploded from his face. At once, he realized that he had failed in his charge so miserably that he could never atone for his errors. It was then that he made his most serious error. For he had forgotten the reason that Gentle White Bear was so called. He had forgotten about forgiveness, for in these four summers, he had never forgiven anyone who had failed in his orders.*

*"Where is my bow? Where are my arrows? Where is my knife? Why do you eat from the elk, when my people are hungry?" Gentle White Bear asked.*

*Limping Dog stammered out that the knife had been stolen and the bow lost in a raid. But as Gentle White Bear looked at him, it became obvious even to Limping Dog that his lies were fruitless attempts to hide.*

*He had taken the things of Gentle White Bear and had treated them with disrespect. He had used them for things that they were not meant to be used for and had ruined the clan's health and power through his selfishness and greed for his own power.*

*"What will you do to me?" he asked. "Will you kill me?"*

*"I will not kill you, Limping Dog," whispered Gentle White Bear.*

*"What then shall be my punishment?" he stammered.*

*"I will no longer be your friend or your brother," Gentle White Bear responded. "You have proven to me and all the others of this clan that you are not a friend to me. You have taken what I have given you and abused it and nearly ruined every-*

*thing. I will have to work for four more summers to put things right. You may not help me. Not I, nor anyone who is a friend to me, will be a friend to you."*

*Limping Dog sat suddenly and heavily with a thump upon realizing his fate, and that he deserved this fate.*

*The one person whom he had looked up to his entire life had disowned him. He knew that he had failed. He also knew that he had failed because he had not tried to become like the one he admired. He had tried to use his power for his own reasons instead of for the reason it had been given to him. He had ruined the property of the Gentle White Bear when it had been entrusted to him for safekeeping.*

*Outside the lodge, the clan had gathered. When Gentle White Bear came out, there was a hush. They had heard what he had said to Limping Dog, and now feared that they too would be banished from the village.*

*"Do not be afraid. Be thankful. You have realized your errors, and I forgive you."*

*But one among them said, "But Gentle White Bear, what have we done? It was you that gave Limping Dog the authority over us. We only did his bidding. Did we not do as you wished?"*

*Gentle White Bear was angered by this. "You, and you alone, are responsible for your footprints along the red road. Limping Dog was placed into power by my authority, but it was you who kept him there. You knew me as well as he did. Why did you not throw him out when he began to lead where you knew I would not take you?*

*Do not try and place all blame on others for your failings. Do not hide from your responsibilities. Stand up and accept that your failings are yours alone, and your successes are what are to be shared with the others who helped you. Because you tried to hide behind Limping Dog, you too are no longer my friend."*

*After saying these things, Gentle White Bear took the rest of the clan and began to rebuild his village. Limping Dog and the one who had denied blame crept into the forest and even today, if you listen closely, you can hear them saying "It was your fault for letting me do wrong," and the quick reply, "No, it was yours for leading us poorly."*

The young man had paid close attention to the story. At its end, he spoke, "That was a good story, but what does it have to do with toys? And why do you call it the story of the broken arrow?"

"The arrow serves many purposes. It is customary to give a young child a special arrow called a spirit arrow. This arrow is made for the child to help guide him on his path. It is straight and true like the red road of life. It is decorated with symbols to remind the child of the way to remain on his path and not get lost.

"The arrow that the Great Spirit has given us is here in the whispers of nature. And we have broken it.

"Toys are simply special things that belong to the pure minds and hearts of children. In our lives, the toys change as we grow, but the toys we play with are still those things that give us the most pleasure in our past times. Gentle White Bear in this story is like the Great Spirit who gave his favorite possession to us his children who are like Limping Dog."

The Fat Man asked, "What is the gift given to us?"

"The Earth, and all its creatures, has been given to us to care for. It is the favorite possession of the Great Spirit. He has labored long and hard to make it perfect.

"In his absence, we are allowed to play with it, but we had better be careful not to ruin it as did Limping Dog. For one day, when the Great Spirit returns, he will recognize us as poor caretakers of His broken earth. And He will no longer call us His friends. And those of us that sit idly by while others ruin this land will fare no better than will the one who tried to hide behind the foolishness of Limping Dog."

"Before you started," said the first man, "you said this story was just perfect for the four of us. Why did you pick this story for us?"

The Earth Warrior looked at the fat man and said, "You are a trading man. In your trading, you take from the earth more than you need, and you do not give back or even heal the wounds of the earth created by your workers. You have broken the possessions given to your care by the Great Spirit."

Looking at the first man, he said, "You are a teacher. Yet you do not teach the people to take care of their borrowed earth. You only teach them to take advantage of the things that aren't even theirs. Do you not think that the Great Spirit will be angry when He returns and sees what we have done to His creation? Is it not your responsibility to show your pupils a better way?"

Looking to the handsome young man searching for the festival toys, he said, "And you are a lawmaker. You are perhaps the worst because it is you that makes up the lies to pretend that all of these things are acceptable and then writes laws to protect the foolish instead of righting these wrongs."

The lawmaker complained, "But should we not be able to use this earth? If, as you say, it was given to us for our care, it is ours to use as we please. Ours to use its resources to make life better for our children."

"And now you are like the complainer in the story," said the Earth Warrior. "You make excuses for your irresponsible actions. It is of course true that you must take what you need just as the hunter takes the buffalo.

"The buffalo was given to the earth for many reasons. One, but only one of these, was to provide meat for us to eat. But to kill the buffalo and then throw away all but the meat is wasteful.

"All the parts of the buffalo are for us to use, and if we use all of what we take, we won't need to take extra to make up for what we waste. To not take all of the buffalo would mean that the other reasons the buffalo are here will be unfulfilled.

"Our greed will only sacrifice the needs of others."

"How are we damaging this earth?" they whined almost in unison.

"I am not hurting anything," said the woman. "I just care for the cabin. I have told these men to be more respectful of the earth."

"Even you that want others to save their forests have not yet learned to care for your own," he said.

Looking at them all, he continued.

"Even your cabins are blights upon the land. Do you not rip out every tree and bush and plant grass stolen from another place? Do you not kidnap bushes from other places in the world and force them to live in soils that are not good for them? Do you not steal flowers from afar and bring them to a place where they live as in a prison?

"Do you not kill the four-legged people of the earth that dare to live near your cabins? Why can you not learn to enjoy the earth as it has been given to you? Do you think that your creations will be better than those the Great

Spirit has given us? Why do you expect others to save their forests, when you cannot even save a single backyard?"

"Do you not know that there are those among you that are able to do these things? There are those that are able to live in harmony with the earth, taking only what is needed and care for the land as the Great Spirit has asked. It is their success that will make your greed even more foolish."

The Earth Warrior was now rested and rose to leave.

Shocked by the outcome of the story, the four travelers looked at each other. Finally, the teacher spoke, "Well, that wasn't as good of a story as I thought it would be."

The others nodded their agreement, but each remained deep in thought about the story.

Passing the small boy on his way back to the path, the Earth Warrior gazed down at him knowing he had overheard the entire story.

"I liked it," he said.

"I thought you would," smiled the Earth Warrior.

# The Nature of Man

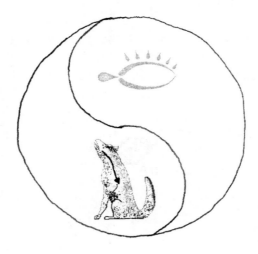

There was a day that the Earth Warrior had paused along his path. Early that morning he had wandered deep into the forest. It was a day that he had wanted to become lost.

After a few hours, he had turned himself around so many times that he did not know exactly where he was. He had to do this by being careful not to pay attention to where he was going. On this morning, he used a trick on himself that had worked before.

As he entered the woods, he caught sight of a remarkably pretty butterfly. He locked his gaze onto it and followed it wherever it led him. As he spotted another butterfly he would stare at it and follow the new leader. After about ten butterflies or so, and not paying attention to where he was being led, the Earth Warrior found himself in a new place.

You may be wondering why he would do such a thing.

Well, a long time ago, the Earth Warrior had learned that the two-legged people are very likely to develop habits. They do things the same way over and over again. This is a fairly good idea when it comes to some things like putting up your tepee. But it can be a very bad idea for an explorer who wants to find new places to see.

And so it was that the Earth Warrior had noticed that he always seemed to walk around a large tree by going to the left side. In reaching a fork in the trails he followed, he always seemed to take the path that seemed to go uphill more than downhill.

He had learned that by allowing himself these habits, he was probably not seeing everything that there was to see and, therefore, was not learning everything that the woods had to teach.

By playing his game with the butterflies, he let himself be led to the tops of the hills and to the bottoms of the swamps. He ended up in briar patches, meadows, on islands in the river. Once he nearly fell off a cliff.

From each of these games of follow-the-leader, he had gained a new insight into the imagination of the Great Spirit. With each of these, he became a better Warrior. Today he had learned the lesson of the burning swamp. But that is another story.

And so now, he relaxed in the grass beside the road and followed the clouds on their journey through the skies.

It was this state of partial meditation that was interrupted by the two hunters coming down the road. They were having a discussion of their morning's hunt. One of the men, the younger of the two, seemed to be rather upset.

He could hear them as they arrived at the meadow where the Earth Warrior lay relaxing, but he did not hear them depart.

Knowing that they had stopped, he sat up and invited them to join him. The two men approached and seated themselves by the Earth Warrior. As was customary in any greeting, they offered to share what they had for food.

Finally, after all three had eaten, they gave their problem to the Earth Warrior. Elder spoke first, as is fitting, "We were hunting the rabbit and the raccoon. We would have taken a small deer if she were to come by. After a time with no luck, this Young One shares with me what his woman partner has said lately. We could hunt no more as our mouths would not stay still long enough to sneak up on a rock. The hunt was over, and we are without meat."

Elder paused. But even though he was not speaking, Young One knew that he had not finished his thought and kept quiet.

"The woman of this Young One," Elder continued, "has told him that she thought it was cruel to kill the rabbit and that we should eat meat no more. She has said that we should no longer wear the skins of the buffalo. We should no longer make our candles from the fat of the bear.

"She has told him that we should live in huts of mud and eat only maize and roots. His woman said to him that she saw the spirits of all of the animals of the earth in a dream.

"Each of these spirits had taken her to their homes and showed her how hard it was to raise their young and feed their offspring. They showed her how they had to dig in the dirt for their food. They showed her the dangers they must face each day from the hunter. And she was filled with pity for them."

As Elder concluded, the Earth Warrior rose. "You must take me to this woman at once."

Rising, the other two were shaken by the seriousness of this response and led him down the path to their village.

Along the way, Young One could not resist his question, "Is my woman right? Should we hunt no more?"

The Earth Warrior said quietly, "You carry the answer in your head every day, and yet you do not know it."

At this, Young One ceased his questioning and pondered the answer. Elder did too but tried not to show it.

Once at the village, the Earth Warrior seated himself by the cooking fire.

"Do you not wish to go into the lodge?" asked Young One.

Elder took Young One's arm. "If he did, he would have. Go and ask your woman to join him here."

As the young woman arrived, the others in the village began to gather around as well, for each of them knew the vision of the woman, and each of them had been shaken into considering what she had said.

The young woman, now called Friend to the Animals, sat. Earth Warrior indicated that Elder should join them. The three of them sat around the fire for a little while and shared a pipe of red sage.

The pipe was shared so that each may know to speak the truth freely but without passion. In this way, the three spirits in the circle could see truth clearly and not be fooled by the glow of conviction. The watching crowd was as still and quiet as if they were of stone.

"Tell us of your vision, Friend to the Animals," said the Earth Warrior.

"Two moons before this day, I slept a deep sleep. In the night a raven came to me and carried me off to the forest. There, he showed me how the animals live. Some in their holes in the ground. Some in holes in a tree. Some in nests. Some in the leaves under the blueberry bush. Some in the water.

"Each animal that I saw was with young. The Aphids on the caterpillar food were with young. The antelope, the elk, the snake, the turtle, the fish, and the eagle were all with young.

"And at each visit, a hunter came and killed the mother. Laughing then, the hunter left the dead mother there to rot into the ground."

She hesitated and then went on to say, "I do not have great medicine. I am not a seer of dreams. I am only a messenger. But I cannot see this dream, as any other, than a warning to stop killing the peoples of the woods. To stop killing the peoples of the plains. To stop killing the peoples of the sky and the water.

"And since I have had this dream, I can only think that I have been chosen to carry this message to the people of my village and not to keep it to myself."

After a long silence, the Earth Warrior spoke to Friend of the Animals, "Was there anything else in this dream that you need to speak? Was there anything that was difficult to explain?"

"Yes," she replied, "two things that I have not even spoken to my husband. The first I made no mention of because it made no sense. The raven, when he walked along the ground, left the footprints of the coyote. The second, I made no mention of because it shamed my heart."

She paused. Since no one spoke, she knew she must continue to speak the truth, "The hunters wore no clothes." Having said this, she looked at Young One fearing he might be angry with her for having such a dream.

Young One, however, had learned the importance of the truth many seasons before and smiled at her with the pride of a husband who knows he has a wife who values truth. His smile removed her embarrassment for having had this dream of naked men.

Earth Warrior understood the dream and comforted the woman. "You have indeed been chosen to be a messenger and have done well to tell all of this. Your only error was to interpret this vision without considering the meaning of the footprints and of the hunters with no clothes."

And so it was that the Earth Warrior began to tell all the village the meaning of this dream.

"There are three things here to be told. The first is that this woman has been chosen to be a great friend to the animals. It is the spirit of Nature herself that has chosen her to see so deeply into the lives of the four-legged peoples of the woods, the winged peoples of the sky, and the swimming peoples of the lake. For what purpose she has been chosen is not spoken in this dream. For this choosing is the first of her steps along the red road of the Great Spirit and not her last."

Looking deep into the eyes of Friend of the Animals, the Earth Warrior spoke very seriously, "Go and learn all that you can about these peoples that share our earth, but do not try to change them. Each of them has their place as does each of us. Your path will lead you to a time when you must know their place as well as you know your own. Other than that I cannot say where the Great Spirit leads you.

"You have been chosen to learn these things, and the first lesson is to learn from all that you see. In your vision, you did not understand the strange footprints and the nakedness of the hunters.

"In not taking the time to learn from all of the vision, you became lost in its meaning. And so it will be in the forest. If you see but do not understand, you must wait for your vision to become clear before you tell your story.

"This is the lesson of the footprints. This Raven is Loki telling you that all things are not necessarily as they might seem at first, and you must take care to see all that is before you.

"Some of the lessons that you will learn will be difficult. Mothers die. Children of these dead mothers may starve or be eaten by Cougar. This is the way of Nature. If Cougar had no orphaned antelope to catch, would it not be the young cougar that starves? Which would you choose?

"The Great Spirit has placed each of us here. Do not presume to change what He has done by making new places for us. New places found from incomplete lessons. Do not take such pride in your knowledge to believe that you could make a better place than that which He has made for us.

"As you learn of Nature and learn of the Man People's place in Nature, do not deny the place of Nature in Man. Do not deny the Man Peoples' need to eat the buffalo and the rabbit, for it is our place given to us by the Great Spirit. It is a place that is understood and accepted by the rabbit and the buffalo. The rabbit and the buffalo have learned to have many children so that there will be enough to feed us and also to make more rabbit and buffalo.

"If it were not for the cougar and the two-legged hunter, the rabbit and buffalo would grow so numerous that they would become diseased and starve a horrible death. To die in the place given you by the Great Spirit is an honorable death that comes at the end of the red road.

"And so take great care to learn all of the lessons and not just those that please you.

"This was the second lesson of the dream."

The Earth Warrior was silent for a great while after saying these things. Finally, Elder spoke the thought on all of their minds. "What of the naked hunters?"

Earth Warrior rose and addressed now all of the men and women of the village.

"These naked hunters of this good woman's dream are a warning that there is an evil in the world. It is an evil that is ten times more dangerous than this woman's mistake of wanting to save all of the animals by no longer hunting them."

Looking to the people, he asked for the eldest and youngest of the hunters to step forward. Elder stood immediately. After a long silence, a boy of only twelve summers came into the fire circle.

Earth Warrior looked to the boy first. "Why do you hunt?"

The boy thought for only a moment, "For food for my mother."

Looking to Elder, the Earth Warriors eyes asked the same question.

"It is true," spoke Elder.

"What is it that becomes of the animal that has given up his spirit?" the Earth Warrior asked the boy.

"The spirit of the animal goes to the skies to be with Creator. His skin becomes a moccasin. His teeth are crushed to powder and added to the food of the old women.

His sinew binds the feathers to the shaft of my arrows. His bones are shaped into arrowheads or needles or spear points or other tools. Each part of him serves a purpose."

The boy seemed both afraid that he was being challenged and proud that he had answered well.

Again the Earth Warrior looked to Elder and repeated the question with his eyes.

"It is true," spoke Elder.

Looking to the boy once more, the Earth Warrior asked, "Tell me of your feelings when you complete your hunt."

The boy looked worried. Since he was inside the fire circle, he knew that he must tell the entire truth. "As I look into the eyes of the rabbit that I will kill, I feel the sadness of the Friend of the Animals. I apologize to the rabbit for his death. The rabbit knows that to die in this way has been his destiny from the day he was born. His spirit apologizes to me for my pain in killing him. I promise him that I will not make any waste of his life and will use all of him for good things.

"I also feel glad that this rabbit will bring a full stomach to my little sister who is only four summers. She is a good sister and someday will make a good mother. But if she is not fed well, she cannot grow strong and might not be taken for a wife. Her children will be weak and sickly and a burden to her and the tribe. And again I thank the rabbit for my sister and her children."

For a third time, the Earth Warrior looked to Elder and repeated the question with his eyes.

"The boy has spoken the truth," spoke Elder.

The Earth Warrior looked to the entire village. "The eldest and the youngest hunter among you know that each hunt is but a single step along the red road of the Great

Spirit. It is your place to provide for your family through the bounty of the land.

"The eldest and the youngest hunter among you know that the hunt is not a game to play. It is not done for pleasure, but pleasure can come from it."

"The evil in the naked hunters is that these men hunt only for their own pleasure. These evil men only pretend to be hunters.

"In fact they are killers sent by evil spirits. While they disguise themselves as hunters, they are made naked by their actions. They did not claim the carcass of the dead animals of the forest. They left them to rot. This killing makes the pure of heart, such as this young Friend to the Animals, hate all of the hunters for the actions of these few.

"In this way, we could all become lost. But learn this lesson. It is not the hunting or the hunters that Friend to the Animals despises. It is the selfishness of the naked hunter.

"Selfishness lies along the yellow path of the seventh direction and is to be cast away. Providing meat and tools for your village lies along the red road of the Great Spirit and is to be honored.

"In remembering that the yellow path of the seventh direction is one for change and that the red path of the Great Spirit is one for acceptance, we can find the truth. But that is another story."

And so the Earth Warrior ended his visit. Elder and Young One walked with him a little way down the path.

After some time, Young One asked, "What did you mean when you said that we carried the answer in our head every day?"

The Earth Warrior stopped and looked at the men. "Do you have the teeth of a goat? Do you have the teeth of the cougar? The Great Spirit does not give us tools that we do not need. And he expects us to use those that we have been given. To do less would be to dishonor Him."

And he left them.

# The Seventh Direction

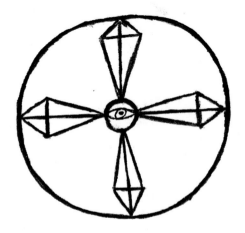

The Earth Warrior had joined the festival on the second day. It was autumn, the time of harvest. All the nearby villages had sent members of their tribes to come and honor the Spirit of the Grasslands in gratitude for his gifts.

For three days, there were to be council fires each night. The drums would play. The dancers would dance. Many stories would be told.

During the daytime, the members of the different villages would sit and visit with each other and trade their goods. These festivals were only held every three moons and so the traders needed to make sure that they obtained all that they could not make themselves in these three days.

When the Earth Warrior arrived, he went to the tepee of his daughter. Winter Blossom had arrived nearly a week ahead of time and had assisted the great old woman who was in charge of this celebration.

After he had placed his things in her tepee, he was told by Winter Blossom that there was to be a special celebration that night. It was a special day, for it was one young man's twelfth autumn and he was to be honored that night. The father had asked the Earth Warrior to join them.

For the rest of the day, the Earth Warrior wandered through the jumble of tents, huts, tepees, and lodges looking at the new crafts. Occasionally he would be asked for a story or to make a decoration for someone's hair. All together, it made for a good day of meeting new people and old friends.

That evening, he sat in the lodge where the young boy was to be honored. Winter Blossom cooked fresh prairie chicken and taro.

"What do these friends of yours expect from me tonight?" he asked his daughter.

"I am not certain. They have not met you, and you have not met them. I think you should just be yourself and see what happens," she answered.

Her advice sounded familiar because it was the same thing that he had told to her so many times over the years—and he took her reminder to heart.

As the evening began, he found a spot near the wall of the lodge away from the door and made it his own. Because he did not know the others in the group, and many were from other tribes, he found himself strangely quiet. He spoke very little as he observed the evening.

Most of the customs were new to him, but he was able to participate at the right moments. The ceremony began with the meal that Winter Blossom had cooked, and then the pipe was lit. Speeches were made by all of the men who were related to the young man, and finally, the father gave him his man's name.

In this tribe, at the age of twelve, boys were to give up the name they were called as a child and take a man's name from their father. This one named his son Heart of the Cougar. This was an unusual name for the Earth Warrior to hear. The evening ended with the father granting the son one wish. On this night though, the son asked to be allowed to dream his wish and ask it in the morning.

While this was an unusual request, it was granted.

The next morning, the father greeted the Earth Warrior as he arose, "My son has asked his wish and I alone cannot grant it," he said.

"What is it that is needed?" replied the Earth Warrior.

"My son has asked that you show him the yellow road," spoke the father. It was fairly obvious to the Earth Warrior that the father was at once honored and offended. He was honored to have this great warrior show this to his son and offended that his son had not asked this gift of his father.

"I will try," spoke the Earth Warrior, "but surely you know that unless you have prepared him well, he will not see it."

The father knew that the Earth Warrior had paid him a great compliment and was relinquishing all credit should he be successful in granting his son's wish. Heart was gladdened by this, for he knew then that the Earth Warrior was likely to succeed.

"We will begin at noon," said the Earth Warrior. "Please have your son meet me by that old hickory tree in the meadow." And so saying, they parted.

At noon, the boy arrived at the tree and found the Earth Warrior already sitting in the grass beneath it. The boy stopped a little way away and watched as the Earth Warrior sat staring at a hickory nut on the ground in front of him.

The Earth Warrior, without looking up, motioned the boy to come closer but quietly.

Heart of the Cougar wondered how the Earth Warrior had known that he was even nearby. He crept closer and saw that the hickory nut was the scene of a terrific battle.

A grub, burrowing safely in the center of the nut, had been exposed by the gnawing of a squirrel. Now an army of ants was attacking this hapless grub. He tried several tricks including spitting up a vile-looking brown fluid that stuck to the ants' legs and made it hard for them to get around, but eventually the little ants overpowered the huge grub and carried him off in little pieces to their tiny caverns.

"What is it that you seek, Heart of the Cougar?" asked the Earth Warrior.

"I seek the way to the yellow road," he answered.

"Sit down and tell me what you have learned so far," said the Earth Warrior nodding to the hickory nut.

This surprised Heart of the Cougar for he had not even realized that his lesson had begun. He said this to the Earth Warrior.

"Your lessons began twelve harvest festivals ago. It is only those that you chose to see as lessons that you have learned thus far. The first thing to accept today is that the lesson is never-ending." The Earth Warrior paused.

"What do you mean," said Heart of the Cougar, "by, *what I must accept?*"

"Some things," replied the Earth Warrior, "are true whether you choose to learn them or not. And this is the way of life. The lesson goes on in every moment. Accept that without question, and you will more easily see the lessons placed before you by the Spirit of the Owl."

"Did you not see the grub and the ants?" he continued. "What was their lesson for you?"

Without waiting for a reply, he continued. "You say that you seek the way to the yellow road. I cannot show it to you. It is a road to which one cannot be led. For no one knows where it begins for any other. But it is a road that even the greatest of fools can find on their own."

"Where is your bow?" Earth Warrior asked.

"Here. I have it," came the reply.

"Stand," the Earth Warrior said, "and shoot an arrow into your target."

"What shall I shoot at?" came the question.

"Shoot," the order was repeated.

And so, Heart of the Cougar chose a small weed on the other side of the shade of the tree and fired an arrow into it.

"What did you learn?" Earth Warrior asked. "You chose a target of your own will. Why did you choose this weed over another? Why did you not choose the mourning dove in the bush next to the weed? Why did you not choose the log? Why did you choose to shoot at all instead of questioning me more?"

Without waiting for an answer, he began again, "Close your eyes. Be still. What do you hear? What can you feel? How many ants are on your left moccasin?"

"Place another arrow in your bow. Now shoot the weed again. Be careful that you make a good aim. Do not open your eyes."

Heart of the Cougar's mind reeled from one question to the next and finally to his quiver where he selected another arrow. He placed it in his bow and fired at the memory of the weed.

He desperately wanted to open his eyes and see if he had come close to the weed, but he dared not.

"Do you hear the squirrel?"

Heart of the Cougar nodded.

"Shoot it."

Heart of the Cougar tensed and listened for the sounds again. He raised his bow. He hesitated. Again the sound came. He loosed his arrow. The silence that followed told him that he had missed.

"Stop. Sit. Be perfectly still."

Heart of the Cougar sat in the grass and waited for the next command. It did not come for a long time.

His mind reeled with questions. These included the ones you might expect about what it was that was happening, and what it was that he was supposed to learn.

But they also included questions about the sounds that he heard: the far off noise of the festival, the nearby snap of a twig, the rustle of the leaves. There were questions about other things: the many smells, the feeling of the bugs crawling on his leg, the dampness of the earth, and how that made it feel cool.

Slowly these last questions became answers. He could feel the hooks on the foot of the bug and guessed it was a beetle of some sort. He could tell that the sun was on his back now when he was in the shade before, so it must be getting late in the day. The smells could be identified. There were the blueberry bush, the oak tree, and the yellow topped weeds. The feeling of the breeze was easy. The squirrel was back.

"Open your eyes. What did you learn?"

Heart of the Cougar had immediately sought to see where his arrow had fallen. When the question was asked, he did not know which to answer first. He began slowly, "I learned—"

"Don't tell me what you learned," interrupted the Earth Warrior. "The answers are not for me. They are for you."

"How will I know if I reached the correct answer?" responded Heart of the Cougar.

"How will I know?" asked the Earth Warrior. "I did not feel what you felt or hear what you heard, or smell what you smelled, or think what you thought.

"My eyes were open, and I played with the butterfly while you sat there. You are the only one who can know if you have arrived at the correct place.

"Try it again."

This time, Heart of the Cougar relaxed himself and sat beneath the tree. His mind soon wandered from the physical things that touched him to the lessons of his youth. Some he had learned well, and some he had chosen not to learn. Some of these were not learned out of stubbornness, some out of a sense of anger, some because he was young and not interested.

But now, somehow as he reflected on these things, he began to remember his frivolity and saw how it had gotten in the way of his lesson. He remembered some lessons that he had never even learned.

He began to think of the things that he could have done differently or better. He thought of some that he could have done worse, and he was proud of these. He also began to think of what it was that he was intended for in the future? Would he become a warrior, a keeper of herbs, a medicine man, a chief, a hunter? Should he choose this thing or should he let his spirit guide show him his place?

And now the questions were getting harder again, so he opened his eyes. It was full night and completely dark. He had sat there with himself for the rest of the afternoon. The Earth Warrior, however, was right there with him.

"Tell me about the yellow road," Heart of the Cougar said to the Earth Warrior.

Nodding, he began, "The yellow road is the road that leads from childhood to the red road of the Great Spirit. Unless you travel the yellow road, you cannot find the beginning of the red road.

"Along this road you will seek many things. Among these are confidence, respect, responsibility, accomplishment, pride, pain, discipline, failure, success, forgiveness, tolerance, perseverance, quitting, letting go, anger, rejection.

"The way to the yellow road is the same for everyone and is different for everyone. The way to the yellow road is to follow the seventh direction."

Seeing the look of not knowing on the face of Heart of the Cougar, the Earth Warrior continued.

"The direction of the rising sun is the first direction. It is our future. The direction of the frozen lands is the second direction. It is preparation. The direction of the warm waters is the third direction. It is the direction of nurturing. The direction of the setting sun is the fourth direction. It is the direction of completeness.

"The direction of the eagle is the fifth direction. It is sight. The direction of the earth is the sixth direction. It is the direction of foundation.

"And the seventh direction—the way to the yellow road—is the direction of *in*. Of self. Of self-knowing. Follow it and tell yourself the truth about your self, and you will find the yellow road and the way to the red road of the Great Spirit. It is this journey that is the journey of life."

And so saying, the Earth Warrior rose to leave.

"Wait," called Heart of the Cougar. "How will I know if I am on the right path? Who will guide me?"

The Earth Warrior smiled "You will know. You will be your own guide. It is your life. You are responsible for it. Enjoy it."

# The Road to a Restful Spirit

There was a time in the life of the Earth Warrior when he had been faced with many troubles. These challenges had caused him to be hungry, and for his children to be hungry. They had caused him to have few possessions. They had caused him to wander the plains and the forests seeking the answers to his difficulties.

At the deepest point of his troubles, he was found one day by the Spirit of the Past. She came to him as an old woman and sat with him for a time.

They talked for a while about all of the things that had happened. During their conversation, she noticed that in spite of all the unhappy things that had happened in the life of the Earth Warrior over the past five winters, he was happily certain that tomorrow would bring him a more comfortable time.

And even though he wished for an easy summer for himself and his children, he was perfectly comfortable having nothing at all. He had no regrets for his choices. He had no anger for those that had harmed him.

As the Old Woman marveled at the composure of this gentle and passive one that called himself a warrior, she was joined by the Spirit of the Future. She came to them in the form of a yearling doe.

As she arrived, a spell came over the Earth Warrior so that he could not see his future. This Young Doe was always very careful to not let herself be seen too clearly by those whom she met. The Earth Warrior would remember her as in a dream. The dream would be pleasant but meaningless.

"Why is that you marvel at this warrior's composure?" she asked the Old Woman, "Is it not the past that you have walked through with him that has given him this gift?"

The Old Woman replied, "What you say is true, but this one has been very severely challenged and he does not waiver from the red road. Try as I might, I cannot see from where in his past he gets this strength."

"Let us put him to the test," the Young Doe answered. Turning to the Earth Warrior, she gave him this thought. "In your future will come a young man. He is to be the next Earth Warrior. You must train him in all of the things that you have come to rely upon in your battles with the evil spirits of the earth. Show him the way of the red road."

Turning to the Old Woman, the Young Doe spoke these words, "Give the young man the innermost memories of the Earth Warrior so that he will be put to a good test."

The Old Woman answered, "I can do that, but I can only give him the thoughts and memories up to the time that the Earth Warrior finds the red road. For once on the red road, all of his inner self is bonded to the Great Spirit and to Him alone. These I cannot see."

And so saying the two spirits took themselves off to a distance where they could see but not be seen.

The Earth Warrior awoke from his dream of the talking doe. He felt easy about his dream but still was confused. For while he knew that the doe had spoken to him, he could not recall a word she had said. To forget so easily was unusual for this warrior.

Soon afterwards, a young man of twenty summers came down the path and stopped before the Earth Warrior.

"I am lost," he said, "is it possible for you to help me find my way?"

The Earth Warrior looked at the young man and knew the words he could not recall. He didn't actually remember the words, but he remembered the feelings that the words carried. He felt the excitement of helping a new person to find the red road. He felt the relaxation of knowing his time as a warrior might soon be over. It was soon to be that time when the Spirit of Hope had told him that he could become a painter of tepees. And he had looked forward to that time.

"Where are you going?" he asked the young man.

"I do not know. I seek my future. I seek to become a warrior for all of the peoples of the earth. I do not know the way."

The Earth Warrior looked deeply into the young man's heart and spirit. "Sit with me," he spoke with a quiet calmness. But his thoughts were troubled by the fact that his vision could not see the pink sparkle of Hope in this young man. His appearance to the eyes was clear and good. But his appearance to the vision of the heart was like looking up at himself from the bottom of a clear lake. He could see his own image standing over the water and looking in, but it was transparent and shimmering in the manner of a lost spirit in the night of the full moon. He knew that this young man before him was not to become a warrior. He knew that he himself was not yet to become a painter. He knew that this young man was given to him as a test. He was not certain from whom the test came, but he detected no evil in it and so determined to go along.

"Do you know the seventh direction?" the Earth Warrior asked.

"I have followed the yellow road for only a long time," replied the young man. "I do not know if I have traveled it to its end or if I have traveled it well."

"Tell me what you have learned," the Earth Warrior asked of this memory of himself.

The young man began a long story of his travels along the yellow road.

*It was the day that I found the seventh direction that I began my travels. I quickly learned that this was a rocky road, and have scars on my feet to prove this is true. Looking closely at these rocks, I could see that each one was not so much a stone, but was a small piece of myself. I learned that I could move these stones around on the path. I was able to arrange these so that their flat sides were up, and my feet had a smooth surface to walk upon. This was very hard work. I found myself wanting to give up, but I persisted.*

*Some of these stones had no smooth surfaces. These were the stones of hatred. The stones of prejudice. The stones of intolerance. The stones of greed. The stones of arrogance.*

*These stones were not desirable in any place on my path. I found that with a great effort, I could throw these stones completely off of this yellow road. There were many of these stones and some were disguised, hiding under stones that I wanted to keep. But by moving every single stone in the path, I was able to find a great many of these and remove them. It took many years to do this task, but then my path was clear and smooth and was much easier to travel upon.*

*In arranging the stones that I kept, and from the spirit guides along the way, I learned many things.*

*I found confidence in the Spirit of the Goat. The teachers of my childhood had told me that confidence is a simple recognition of one's own ability. It is much more than that. True confidence is in using the ability gifted by the Great Spirit to do the work of the Great Spirit. True confidence, like the goat hopping from crag to crag in the mountain, is a combination of our talent, our training, and the guiding hand of the Spirit.*

*I found resilience in my meeting with the Spirit of the Lizard. Like the lizard that loses his tail, when we are dealt a loss by the Spirits of Challenge, we must go on being who we are, like the lizard goes on being a lizard. After a time, we will recover just as the lizard grows a new tail.*

*I found respect in meeting the Spirit of the Snake that Rattles. He and I found that if we had respect for each other, I would not come too close, and he would not threaten me. From this respect, we found that we did not need to be enemies. I respect him for his nature, and he respects me for mine. We do not attempt to change each other or to kill each other.*

*There is also the lesson of tolerance that I learned from the Spirit of the Great Ocean Turtle during my visits to the South and the Land of the Warm Waters. The great turtles swim in the sea for a hundred years and carry the barnacles on their backs. These barnacles do no good for the turtle, but neither do they do harm. The turtle does not attempt to scrape them off or to rid himself of them. He accepts them as they are. The barnacles, in their turn, do not attempt to tell the turtle where to swim. They simply accept the ride and do not try and direct it.*

*Responsibility I took from my meeting with the Spirit of the Cougar. Mother Cougar takes a great deal of time in caring for her cubs. She sacrifices herself to bear them and then to feed them. She teaches them the ways of the mountains and the plains so that they will be able to survive when she is gone from them. Father Cougar may seem as if he has no responsibility, for he leaves Mother Cougar and cubs alone. In his own way, though, he accepts that Mother Cougar is capable of this job and to interfere would be nothing more than a bothersome distraction for her and the cubs. This is not true for all of the mothers and fathers of the four-legged peoples. The lesson I learned is that responsibility can come in many forms.*

*Understanding I learned from the Spirit of the Fox. Only the Fox seems to learn so many of the habits of his prey that he can be where they will be before they arrive.*

*I learned trust from the Spirit of Flying Squirrel. How is it that the young squirrel leaps from his perch for the first time? He has no feathers like the winged peoples of the sky. He leaps only because Mother Squirrel assures him it will be all right. He leaps out of trust.*

*Pride was taught to me by the Spirit of the Vulture. In the air, this graceful bird flies high above even the eagle. He rises in the morning to great heights without even a single flap of his wings. The circles in the sky are easily made. And yet this proud bird with his naked head is ugly and clumsy when seen up close and eating the dead meat that another had to kill for him.*

*It was Iktomi the Spider that taught me discipline. This little spider weaves his web time and time again. Each time it is woven, it is the same as the last. When the web is broken, you do not hear the spider complain. The strands of the broken web have not even fallen to the ground before the little spider has begun to weave it again.*

*Failure was given to me as a gift by the Spirit of the Beaver. The beaver works all summer long to build his pond in the stream. When the rains of the spring or the ice of the winter break down his work, he accepts it as easily as he accepts the water on his back. Failure for the beaver is not a loss to be mourned. It is a chance to build again.*

*The Spirit of the Stallion taught me the lessons of leadership. The stallion, of all of the leaders of the animals that travel together, is the only one that leads from the front. That is to say, it is the stallion that will leap the arroyo before he asks his mares to do so. It is the stallion that will charge the cougar before his mares join in. It is the stallion that drinks first from the pond to make sure that the water is sweet.*

*Partnership, even the partnership that comes in the man-woman partner, was the lesson of the Spirit of the Pheasant. The pheasant only flies short journeys over the prairie. On arising from the grass, the wings of the pheasant move tremendously fast. And yet they move at exactly the same time. In gliding to rest, the wings are held as still as death. A pheasant with only one wing cannot lift both sides of her body. Even so, each wing is exactly the opposite of the other. It is the partnership of these wings that allows the pheasant to avoid the fox. And while her flight is short, taken together, they can make a lifetime of partnership.*

*It was these stones in the yellow road that I kept and placed so that I would have a smooth path.*

*I found that building my yellow path of these stones and removing the others had given me a quality that others that I meet call* character.

*I found that having worked so hard on this path, I learned to value my own opinion of whether a particular stone was placed correctly or not. I found that I still valued the opinion of others in these matters, but that the responsibility for the final decision was mine. In this way, I found that my character was the way that I wanted it to be and not a confused mixture of false attempts to please others.*

*Having spent much time arranging these stones, I found that I could walk a little bit down this yellow road. In doing so, I learned even more lessons of the yellow road.*

*I learned of pain. I learned that pain is the spirit's way of telling us that not all things are right. A pain in the heart, a pain in the spirit, or a pain in the body can be lessened through the simple act of accepting it. This is not to accept blame or fault or even to accept that what caused the pain cannot be made to go away. It is only to accept things as they are for the time that they are.*

*I learned of success. I learned it was seldom mine to claim. My successes were only the result of using the tools that the Great Spirit had gifted me at my birth to accomplish a task that He had placed before me. The only success that I could claim was in recognizing the task and in persisting in my work.*

*Forgiveness was the fruit of the marriage of the lessons of tolerance and of pain. By learning to accept pain and to tolerate others for not being those whom I would have them be and for not making the choices for themselves that I would have made for me, I found forgiveness. And from knowing forgiveness, I found that I had released my spirit from the need to find any fault or to place any blame when the wind did not blow at my back. For, I asked, "Where is the need to spend time and energy figuring out exactly who is to blame if it is only to forgive them?" In this way, forgiveness frees the spirit to seek other things. And so it was that blame and fault were stones I flung from the yellow road.*

*And then, after learning these things, the lessons of the yellow road began to behave like the pine cone dropped on the winter mountain. This small seed pod falls from the tree and strikes the snow, loosening it. The snow slides down the mountain and loosens more snow. It is not long before the entire white mask falls away revealing the face of the mountain.*

*I learned that to be overpowered by an adversary was not a cause for shame. It was a lesson to be used in avoiding being beaten the next time.*

*I learned that perseverance can be a good substitute for skill. This is especially so if the time used in perseverance is also used to learn the lessons that the lack of skill may teach. I learned that just as certainly as losing a struggle is not a cause for shame, to quit of one's own accord is nothing less than to throw away all of the gifts of the Great Spirit. It is to throw away His trust in you and your trust in Him. And so it was that I threw away these stones in the yellow road. In seeking out these stones of quitting, I learned that there is a similar stone that is to be kept. It is the ability to be able to let go of a false task. If we are sometimes imperfect in our ability to see the tasks placed in front of* us by the Great Spirit, we can forgive ourselves the error and let go of an unworthy pursuit.

And in this lesson, I found the stone that fit between the cobbles of fate and the cobbles of my free will that ran down the edges of my yellow road. I had hopped from one side of the path to the other over the vacant ground in between. For many moons, I could find no stones that would fit into this part of my path. At last, I found a large stone that had, on one edge, the ability to choose, and on the other, the inescapableness of the Spirit of Fate.

And I saw that it was the Spirit of Fate that placed our choices before us, but it was our own spirits that selected our path. It was the strength of our character that allowed us to choose well.

And I learned even more about responsibility than what Cougar had taught. In having our choices only presented to us and in having our ability to choose kept to our own spirits, we must accept that we are totally responsible for each and every thing that happens to us.

It was far down the yellow road that I learned the secrets of anger. I am sometimes embarrassed that I had not seen this lesson earlier when I had learned the lesson of pain. For anger is nothing more than a rejection of pain. Whether the pain is a pain to the spirit or the mind or the body, anger is our way of expressing our desire to not have this pain. And yet, if we accept the pain, it no longer hurts and our anger is not necessary. A part of this is to accept the responsibility as well as the pain. When all of these stones in the road were placed together, it was easy to see that if we accept responsibility for our choices, place no blame on ourselves or others, forgive ourselves our mistakes, and accept the pain of the error, we can dig the stones of anger from the yellow road and throw them into the sea.

*I also learned that this lesson is not to cage the anger some-place within our hearts. That is not the same thing. To do this would be to fill our very spirits with an anger that would eventually blacken our hearts and kill us.*

*I learned these things and found my yellow road to be long but flat and smooth. I found then three more lessons in the stones that remained.*

*I learned that revenge is not a matter of justice. It is an act of both selfishness and disrespect. These stones I had tried to remove many moons before, but I must admit that I still find fragments from time to time.*

*Revenge is selfish because it is not conducted as a punishment on the offensive. It is conducted as a gratification of our own spirits. It is disrespectful because revenge takes from the Great Spirit His rights. Only He has the right to say when a man's spirit is to leave his body. For us to end another's life is to be so disrespectful of the Great Spirit that we would steal this from Him.*

*I found that the rejection that I had experienced by others was not so much their statement that I was somehow inferior, incomplete, or not good enough. It was instead an expression that said the other spirit would have made different choices had the fates presented them with the same situations.*

*And I learned love. No, that's not quite right. I may not yet know love. I am not certain. What I have learned is the absence of hate. But in the absence of hate, and the absence of intolerance, there is a certain acceptance that seems to be what I imagine is love.*

*And after all of this, I find that while I have heard of the red road of the Great Spirit, I cannot find it."*

With these words, the young warrior ended his tale and looked to the Earth Warrior for assistance.

"That is an amazing tale," he said. Of course since it was his own tale, he knew it word for word before the young man had said it. And that made it easier for him to answer. "In spite of all that you have learned, you still look for the red road with your eyes and not your heart. If you do not open your heart, you will never find this road. For it is love that is the first step upon the red road of the Great Spirit." The Earth Warrior rose to leave.

"Wait," cried the young man. "You have not told me what I need to know."

"I do not need to tell you," he replied. "You already hold the answer that you seek."

The two spirits watched from their distance as the Earth Warrior walked slowly down the road away from the apparition.

Soon they fell into an argument over whether he had passed the test or had failed it, forgetting about the third possibility altogether.

# Alone

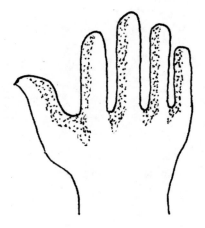

The Earth Warrior walked along his path on a sunny after-noon. The air was clear and the wind was cool.

The forest spoke to him from the North but there was little to distract him. The woods only made conversation. They did not call for his help.

Arriving at a curve in the path, he was filled with admi-ration for the Great Spirit for the curve revealed to him a new view of the land that Creator had made. He had looked up from his feet and away into the distance. As he did so, his foot struck a small stone, and he stumbled.

He stooped to pick up the stone. His spirit was captivated by the colors and cracks of the stone. Sitting down in the middle of the path, he studied the stone, letting their spirits become one and listening for the stories the stone would tell. First he held it one way and then another. Each time he turned it over, the cracks and lines of the rock took on the shape of a different animal.

Each time, each new animal shape spoke to him. Each of the spirit animals of the stone spoke the same words in a different tongue.

He smiled and thought that this simple stone carried the understanding of many things. In this stone was the understanding of the secret that cannot be told but that can be learned by anyone.

Realizing that he had stumbled on it when he had gazed away from his path, another lesson was learned. He arose and began on his way once again. The stone had taught him once again that to gaze away from his path was to stumble. It had reminded him that, once learned, to forget the lesson of the stone was to become lost.

Soon he came to a field where two young boys were playing. They played an ancient game of hoops and stones. Using a simple hoop bent from a willow branch or a grapevine, one boy would throw or roll the hoop. The other would take aim and try to throw the stone through the hoop. On some days, they would use a sling for their stones. On others, they would use their arrows or clubs.

Neither boy marked a stick to account for which one had made more hoops. But each knew which one had the better aim. And knowing so, they did not need to mark the stick.

Seeing the Earth Warrior approach, they fell silent and still. Each of them knew that a new friend approached. Each of them could see that the man on the path was a great warrior.

These boys had been told stories of the ancient Teiwaz and had practiced seeing with their heart and not their eyes alone. The Earth Warrior's presence in the heart was clear and easy for those not blind to see.

The boys approached the Earth Warrior and stood before him. The Earth Warrior could see with his heart that each of them was pure, and he knew that they could see him just as easily. So he decided to stay with them for a while.

The taller boy began to explain their game, saying that they both were soon to be warriors and protect their people. The game was to teach them skills in hunting and agility.

The smaller boy let him finish and then began to ask the warrior how it was that he was the warrior for all people and no people.

"You are the Earth Warrior. We know of you and are glad of your quest. We too would one day protect our people and all of the four-legged people of the woods. We would protect the people of the winds and the people of the waters. Our skills are growing, and soon we will be tested. But one question remains for us to answer. Your answer will be our answer if we are to be true to our path."

The taller boy then spoke, for he was the more accurate with the stones.

"Why do you walk alone?"

The Earth Warrior smiled and motioned them to all sit down. "Let me tell you a story," he said.

*In the land between the great rivers, there lived three young men. These men were brothers of different mothers, and each was known as a great warrior.*

*Together they traveled the path before them. Their paths had not always been the same path, for they were brothers of different mothers. But for many years they had walked together.*

*They had nothing and they wanted for nothing. For at every meal, the spirits provided their food. On every cold night, the spirits provided their shelter. When it was hot, there was water for them to drink. When their bows were old and had lost their power, an orange wood tree was soon found growing even in the middle of the desert. From this they would make new bows. The only thing they provided for themselves was their courage.*

*During their time together, they had performed many feats of strength and gentleness. They had always followed the spirits of their hearts and had developed great strength of character. They were great warriors but not yet warriors of the Teiwaz.*

*One day as they traveled down the path, a great spirit in the form of a dragon appeared to them.*

*The dragon warned them that day. "Soon your test will come. Stay on your path like the arrow flies to its mark." And he vanished. Where he stood was a golden-colored egg with stones of turquoise and obsidian at each end.*

*The youngest of the three picked it up and held it in his hand.*

*"I will keep this egg. I will protect it, and it will bring me great power."*

*The eldest looked at him and warned him to throw it away. But the younger warrior refused, for as soon as he had touched the egg, he had been overcome by the spirit of the magpie. He tried to place it in his pouch, but he realized that it would break. He could only hold onto the egg safely if he held it in his hand.*

*The second warrior secretly wished that he had picked up the egg first.*

*The three went on along their path for three days more. Suddenly, in the path ahead was a young woman of the people from across the little water.*

*A great bear was up on his rear legs before her. The bear breathed his roar into the air that was to be her last breath.*

*The three brothers of different mothers surrounded the bear and began to fight with him. Each of the elder brothers had a knife in his left hand and a club in his right. The younger brother had not let go of his egg and so carried only his knife.*

*The bear turned to face this younger brother and swung a great paw at him. The young warrior instinctively raised his right hand to block the bear's attack. Realizing that he had no club but a precious egg in his hand, he lowered it to save the egg. The young warrior was cut deeply by the claws of the bear. Falling to the ground, he still held the egg safely, for he was a great warrior and had sworn to protect it.*

*The bear disappeared into the woods as the young warrior's life drained from his wounds out into the path.*

*The two remaining brothers and the young woman gave the younger warrior a hero's burial and went along their way.*

*The second younger brother now held the woman's hand in his left hand and the egg in his other.*

*After three more days had passed, there appeared in the path before them a great snake. The snake was about to devour a small child. The child cried to the warriors for help.*

*The elder warrior circled to the right of the snake to distract him from the child. The second younger brother could not decide whether to let go of the hand of his woman or to let go of the egg. As he stood there, the snake coiled and struck him in the chest.*

*Just as the snake sank his fangs into the younger warrior's heart, the elder warrior was able to swing his great knife and cut the snake's head cleanly from his writhing body.*

*The elder warrior then watched as the snake's head turned into a bird and flew away into the south sky. The body of the snake fell apart as it hit the ground. Each part became a thousand tiny snakes that slithered off the path and into the tall grass.*

*The woman stood and watched calmly as these things happened. The child stopped crying. The egg was still safe in the hand of the second brother of different mothers, for he too was a great warrior and had sworn to protect it.*

*The elder warrior then took the egg from the dead brother's hand and gave it to the woman. He placed the hand of the child into her other hand and sent her on her way to the village down the road.*

*When he looked back to the dead brother, he saw that the body had turned from that of a strong young warrior to that of a frail and weak old man. All signs of his former strength and prowess as a warrior were gone forever.*

*Before he could give the body a decent burial, a warm wind came down from the hills and blew his body into dust. The wind carried the dust away into the meadow. There the dust settled, and no more flowers of the prairies ever bloomed there again.*

The Earth Warrior rose to leave.

"Please, stay a moment," spoke the smaller boy. "I do not understand your answer."

The taller boy looked deep into the Earth Warrior's heart.

"The warrior cannot hold a bow or a club if his hands are filled with the treasures of the greedy. One cannot fight to save another if his hand clings to that of a woman. To place one's spirit on the chosen path is to leave all these things behind. To become a warrior one must be willing to give everything one has to the fight. If one has nothing, this can be done. If the warrior carries with him possessions, he will spend his life protecting his own desires and will be unable to help others."

The Earth Warrior smiled the smile of the teacher whose student has only slightly missed the mark.

"What you say is true, young warrior. But you must remember as well that the spirit has no hands or feet. The warrior spirit does not need possessions. And yet, the possessions of the spirit are the most valuable of all.

"You asked how it was that I am the warrior for all people and no people. It is because of the possessions of my spirit that I am able to let go the possessions of my hands.

"The second of the brothers of different mothers held his woman by the hand in order that she may walk with him.

"He had forgotten that none can walk as close as one who walks with the heart."

And the Earth Warrior left, still alone, but with two new companions.

# The Pebble in the Road

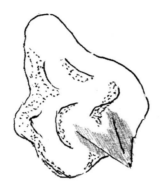

"Grandfather," said the young one, "what is it that is most valuable in your medicine bag?"

The Earth Warrior smiled the smile of an elder and remembered the day he gave this little one's father, White Fox, his medicine bag. He supposed that his story had already been told to this young one.

"All the tokens are valuable, little one, or they would not be there. Is that not true?"

"Yes, grandfather. But does not one have more secrets than the others?" the boy asked with calm persistence.

"Well, there is one item that does have more secrets. So I shall show you." The Earth Warrior opened his medicine bag and began to remove small reminders of his youth. Near the bottom was a small pebble. He put it on one of the rocks that rimmed the fire beside which the two stay. The little one looked closely at it but did not touch. The pebble was a fine pebble indeed. Its milky white surface had been smoothed by years of grandfather holding it and rubbing it. Still, there was a blotch on it which looked a bit like dry blood.

The boy pointed to the darkened area and, smiling quizzically at grandfather, asked, "That is the story, is it not?"

Pleased with the curiosity and the quickness of his son's son, the Earth Warrior nodded. "I suppose you want me to tell you all about it, don't you?" he asked.

The little one smiled and nodded vigorously. "I want you to, but I also know you like to teach me to work things out for myself, for a lesson learned is seldom as well learned as a lesson discovered. So tell me a story so that I may find my own secret in your pebble."

Once again, the Earth Warrior was impressed with this young one. He must remember to compliment White Fox and Silver Deer, his mother.

"Very well. Many summers ago, a young and strong warrior arose from childhood to become very influential in his tribe. There was little cause for this, for while young and strong, the warrior had not yet learned wisdom. As the years passed, his influence grew, but not his wisdom. You see, little one, just as a man exercises with his bow to become strong and accurate, one's spirit must be exercised in order to become wise. A man's spirit holds his character, his honor, and his reason closely together. When challenged, it is these which guide his muscles in battle. Without honor and reason, battle has no purpose."

The Earth Warrior poured a cup of tea and continued. "This warrior, of whom I speak, received many physical challenges but was never faced with a spiritual one. As he grew in strength, he achieved a place in the tribe well above the place of his spirit. One day, as he reveled in a new appointment to the chief hunter of deer, he began to prance about in self-adulation. Singing and skipping, he danced along the road towards the woods where he would find meat for his people.

"His spirit guide, however, had other plans. As the warrior danced, his toe found a small pebble in the road of happiness. All his weight came down on this pebble, and it pierced his foot, causing him to lose his balance. The dancer thumped face down in the path, and he entered the spirit world, if only for a short time.

"His spirit guide came to him as a butterfly. Her wings took her on a dance in the air much like the dance our warrior had been doing on the road. As he watched, the butterfly flew into the side of a tree, then a rock, and, finally attempting to land on the road, she flipped over at the last second and lay there on her back. She struggled against her big wings and finally righted herself, standing on a small pebble.

The warrior looked at her in amazement.

Spirit Guide said, "Get up, if you can."

The warrior jumped to his feet and then fainted.

"Get up," she repeated.

The warrior stood more slowly this time but could not focus his eyes, so he sat again with a thump.

"What is it?" he cried. For now he was beginning to become fearful.

"Who are you?" she asked.

"I am a great warrior and a great hunter. I am strong. I am quiet enough to creep up on a rabbit or a fawn. I am the leader of my hunting party," he replied.

"No," she said. "That is what you are. I asked who you are."

Realizing he did not know the answer, light faded to black, and he fell into darkness.

A little while later, the warrior awoke. He was lying in the road bruised, confused, and with a throbbing toe. Sitting up, he saw a small pebble by his foot and realized what had happened. Picking it up, he was about to fling it into a creek when a butterfly passed before him. Looking at the pebble and remembering his dance, he realized that powerful men are still at the mercy of such things as pebbles in their path.

The warrior dusted himself off and went down the road much more quietly.

The butterfly followed for a while, listening to the warrior ask, "Who am I?" And she knew he was now on the road to wisdom.

# The Other Side
# of the Mountain

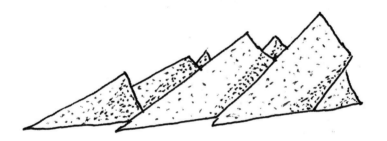

The sun peeked over the prairie, signaling the start of a brisk new day. The men had gathered together before first light to watch. They gazed not at the sun, but to the west where the Mountain burst into reds, greys, blacks, and yellows that chased away the purple of the night. The Mountain was complex, and each rock formation had a peculiar glow in the bright sun. The wise men of the group claimed to be able to read these colors, much as some elders had claimed to be able to see the future in the leaves of tea.

The Mountain spoke to the wise men in this manner, and the Mountain was their god.

In the plains, north of the mountain, another group of men watched as the sun chased shadows sideways across the snowy face of the slopes. Here too, wise men proclaimed that the brightness of the sun, and the speed of the retreat of the shadows was the Mountain's way of telling them that winter was being chased away. The Mountain was telling them to prepare for spring. It would soon be time to plant crops and to harvest the tender young buffalo. The men listened and prepared, for the mountain was their god.

To the west of the Mountain, the men held a festival. They started a bit later in the day and timed it so that the celebration began just as the sun crested the peak. What had been a chilly forenoon was quickly a warm spring day. This was the one day of the year when the sun rose exactly over the highest peak of the Mountain. These men had honored the Mountain since before time, for it had always provided a fresh stream to drink from and much game from its slopes. This day would end with a glowing spectacle of the west face of the Mountain as it was bathed in the golden rays of the setting sun. The men would thank and worship the Mountain, for the Mountain was their god.

South of the Mountain, a group of men gathered to watch the sun stretch the trees into long streaks across the valleys. Their Mountain was green, for the trees were blessed with a southern sun and rains driven up from the plains. The Mountain spoke to the men, telling them to prepare for a spring replete with deer and goats from the forest. The men rejoiced as their wise men told them what the Mountain had said, for the Mountain was their god.

In the fall of that year, the Earth Warrior walked in the prairie to the east of the Mountain. He was distraught. As he walked, he passed the bleached bones of many men and horses. Arrows, clubs, and knives littered the earth. Off in the distance was a single trail of smoke rising into the air. As he drew closer, he saw that it came from a small campfire outside a small tent. On a log sat a young woman and her two children. They were preparing a dinner of rabbit and invited the Earth Warrior to join them, for that was the custom with travelers.

As the dinner was prepared, the Earth Warrior asked the woman about the sights he had seen in the prairie. She wept as she told him of the summer.

As it happened, a warrior from the east side of the Mountain came across a warrior of the south while hunting. Being respectful, they shared the day hunting, and it was not until nightfall that each learned of the failing of the other. They both worshiped the Mountain at nightfall, each praising his god for his fortune. It was only when the southern warrior referred to the Mountain as the green god of life who whispers in the trees that the eastern warrior took issue. He tried to explain that the Mountain was the god of many colors, not just green. It was during this argument that the two heard more argument from across the arroyo. They put aside their differences long enough to seek out two other men in heated debate. These two were from the north and west sides of the Mountain and, in similar fashion, were arguing that the Mountain was the white giver of constant streams or the golden god of the sunset. Soon, all four were arguing. Each set out to get the wise men from his tribe so that it may be settled among the spiritual ones.

The next day, war parties from all four tribes met on the prairie. Wise men from each met in the center, and none would be moved, for each knew his god well. Once the impasse was acknowledged, the warriors found they could not accept the blasphemy of the others, and each set out to kill the others should they not give up their false god.

Soon all were dead or dying of their wounds. The women and children of the four tribes dispersed into the surrounding plains looking for new homes beyond the shadow of the mountain which had betrayed them all.

Only this young one remained, crying, "It was the same mountain."

And this is the story that cannot be taught but which can be learned by all.